BLINDSIDED

ANGELA TAYLOR

Firelite Press LLC

Angela Taylor

Firelite Press LLC
  Middleton, ID 83644

First Firelite Press LLC Paperback Printing: October 2020
  ISBN: 978-1-7354925-0-6

First Firelite Press LLC E-book: October 2020
  ISBN: 978-1-7354925-1-3

DEDICATION

For my father, Paul Simitzes. I was so blessed to have you as my dad. Thank you for always being there for me and for passing on your love of movies, chocolate and wicked, warped sense of humor. I miss you every day. Keep throwing those pennies down, and I'll keep looking up. Love you, Daddy.

For my mother, Diamond Dufenhorst. How lucky am I to have the cool mom? The mom friends used to come over to ask questions they didn't feel comfortable asking their own parents. The mom who instilled my love of animals and taught me how to cook Greek food. Who has gotten me through some of the worst times…and has become my best friend, even though we sometimes drive each other crazy. You are, simply put, the best mom ever. Oh my stars, I love you.

Also, a heartfelt thank you to my dear friend, Janis McCurry, whose advice has been invaluable.

CHAPTER ONE

Holly Richland stopped short on the sidewalk when she heard a splash, followed by the annoying sensation of water seeping into her canvas tennis shoe. She sighed and opened her eyes to glare down at the German shepherd standing on her left side.

"Riley, you're supposed to lead me around the puddles, not through them," she muttered.

It was his second mistake today. Holly believed in his capabilities, but Riley was running out of time as far as Carmen, the director of Guide Dogs of the Rockies, was concerned. After begging and pleading, she'd finally managed to talk Carmen into letting her work with the dog a little longer before he was "career changed" and cut from the program. Fourteen days was all she had left to make Riley into the guide dog she knew he could be. Fourteen days.

"You've got to try a little harder, Riley," she told the dog, squatting down on her haunches to reach his level. "I know you can do it, and you know you can do it, but now we've got to convince Carmen. It's time to prove yourself, kiddo."

The mostly black and tan German shepherd looked her

straight in the eye, as if listening intently, then licked her. She made a face and wiped the back of her hand across her cheek.

"Concentrate," she ordered, actually managing to resist his I'm-so-sorry-but-can't-you-forgive-me-because-I'm-cute look and not scratch him behind his ear like he wanted.

He whined in response to her non-compliance.

"Oh, stop it, you big baby." She straightened, picked up the handle on Riley's harness and informed him, "I'm not falling for it, so let's get back to work." Once again closing her eyes behind the dark sunglasses she wore, she gave the command, "Forward."

Riley started walking, and she followed as soon as she felt the steady pull of the harness. They'd already been over two of their regular routes today. This was the third. Maybe she was pushing him a little hard, but she only had two weeks left. When the time was up, he had to be perfect. Carmen wouldn't settle for anything less.

Riley stopped at a corner, which meant they must have just passed the drug store. She said, "Right" and the dog turned and led her past the police station, toward the park. Once they reached that, she'd let him take a break and—

Holly didn't have time to finish her thought before a tank rammed into her. She stumbled sideways, tripped over Riley, who yelped sharply, and landed on the sidewalk with a thud so powerful it knocked the wind out of her. She gasped for air, but either her lungs had been damaged or she'd forgotten the proper way to inhale, because for the life of her, she couldn't draw a breath. It definitely didn't help with Riley licking her face.

"Hell, lady! Why don't you watch where you're going?"

After scowling at her for a moment, the tank in question held out a hand, but lack of oxygen made it impossible for her to take it. He jerked his hand back, cursed under his breath, then reached down, grasped both of her hands in his huge ones and pulled her to her feet. The abrupt motion must have jump-started her lungs, because suddenly she was inhaling quicker than oxygen poured into a newly opened vacuum-packed can. At last, she could breathe.

"What's the matter with you, anyway?" the tank asked in disgust. "Are you blind?"

She opened her mouth to shout, *No, but you're a complete jerk*, then thought better of it. True, the guy was a jerk. A big jerk. No. More like a huge, towering, built like a brick wall, I-bench-press-cars type of jerk. After all, he ran into her, not the other way around. Somebody needed to teach the guy a lesson, not to mention some manners, and happily that some-body was her.

"Yes, as a matter of fact, I am," she stated flatly, delighting in the way his eyes widened, then filled with shock.

Deliberately his gaze traveled from the dark sunglasses she wore, to the guide dog at her feet, back to her glasses. How she managed not to laugh when the color drained from his tanned face, she'd never know.

"God, I'm...I'm sorry," he stammered. "I didn't know."

"Of course you didn't," she snapped, enjoying herself, "because *you* didn't bother to look where you were going. If you had, you would've at least seen my dog before you plowed into me."

His mouth worked on a silent apology, kind of like a fish gasping for air after it's been taken out of water. She got the impression he wasn't a man used to being at a loss for words; that it made him uncomfortable. Good. Served him right. The man was a menace to society.

She leaned over and made a show of feeling around for Riley's harness before she grasped it in her left hand and picked up his leash in her right. Straightening, she cocked her head toward the man, but deliberately stopped a few inches off of the mark. "Maybe next time *you'll* watch where *you're* going," she said, hoping her tone sounded condescending. "Riley, forward."

She hadn't taken three steps when the guy materialized at her right side. She pretended not to notice.

"I truly am sorry. I've had a hell of a month, and I'm taking it out on you."

"Are you still here?" She shook her head, never slowing her pace. "What? Did you come back to finish me off?"

Riley led her around a break in the sidewalk, and she hid her smile when the man caught his boot on the broken cement and stumbled.

"Let me make it up to you," he pleaded when he was once again next to her.

"No."

"Come on. At least let me buy you a cup of coffee."

She kept walking, but didn't answer him immediately. She had skipped lunch, and it couldn't hurt for Riley to get more practice in an actual restaurant. Besides, she rationalized, sneaking a glance at the large man pacing her, it was kind of fun making him suffer.

"Will you throw in a Danish?"

"Whatever you want."

"Okay. I'll let you buy me a cup of coffee, but you have to tell me your name first."

He grinned. "It's Ash. Ashford Malone."

"My name's Holly, Ashford Malone, and I only like expensive coffee."

∼

A short while later Holly was sipping a creamy *cafe latté* in an extremely expensive gourmet coffee shop. There wasn't room for him under the table, so Riley was lying on the floor behind her chair. Ashford Malone was sitting directly across from her. Since she hadn't taken off her sunglasses, she was able to get a good look at him without him realizing.

He wasn't classically handsome, she decided. His jaw was a little too prominent, and his nose had obviously been broken, maybe more than once. Still, there was something appealing about him. Something unequivocally male that made her feel more feminine than she had in years.

His dark hair was a little on the long, shaggy side. It curled slightly at the ends and dipped beneath the collar of his rumpled T-shirt. His short beard was equally unkempt, but it looked more like he hadn't bothered to shave for a few weeks, rather than deliberately growing it. She couldn't tell if his eyes were blue or green with her sunglasses on.

When he lifted the espresso cup to his lips, she was once again struck by how big he was. She knew the cup was tiny, but the man probably didn't need a mitt to play baseball.

"So," Holly began, using both hands to place her mug on the table. She felt around until her fingers touched her fork, then used it to cut through the sticky apple strudel on the plate before her. It wasn't the easiest feat, since she was trying not to look at it. "Are you one of the good guys or the bad guys?" she asked, slowly lifting the strudel to her lips. It tasted heavenly. Tart and sweet at the same time, with walnuts and raisins and a flaky crust that melted in her mouth.

"Excuse me?"

"Cop or criminal?" she clarified, licking her lips. "I know it could be kind of a personal question, depending on your answer, but you did practically hit warp speed coming out of that police station, and I just—"

"How did you know it was a police station?"

"—figured you were either running after someone or from someone. Since I'm having coffee with you, it probably wouldn't be a bad idea to find out which one it was." She took another bite of strudel, waiting for his reply. When he didn't answer, she realized he'd asked her a question somewhere in the middle of her explanation. She had a terrible habit of turning simple conversation into a verbal avalanche. She really needed to try to listen more and talk less. "What did you say?"

"How did you know it was a police station?" he repeated, apparently unoffended by her rambling.

"Oh." She thought for a moment before answering. "Because of the smell."

"The...smell?"

She nodded. "It smells like crime."

Dead silence.

Watching his slightly worried, definitely puzzled expression from behind the cover of her sunglasses, she kept a straight face for as long as she could manage, then burst into laughter.

"I'm kidding," she informed him between giggles. "I may be blind, but I'm no bloodhound. Your other senses don't sharpen that much."

He wrinkled his thick brows. "Then how did—"

"Familiar route. How else do you think I find anything? I have practically the entire city memorized." Now, that was the truth. She'd been over nearly every inch of Denver training dogs. "I probably know it even better than you do...if you're a cop. Which reminds me, cop or criminal? Are you really going to pay for my coffee, or wait until I do and steal my wallet?"

He smiled then, a full out, ear-to-ear grin revealing perfect, white teeth. Holly got the feeling he never would've smiled like that if he thought she could see him. Maybe the haunted look she'd seen in his eyes earlier was the reason he was so guarded. She could still see the ghost of it now, flickering faintly, refusing to be totally extinguished.

"Cop," he said softly, almost wistfully.

She wondered at his tone, but let out an elaborate sigh nonetheless. "Good, because I didn't bring my wallet."

He laughed, and she experienced an irrational surge of pleasure at having been able to coax it from him. The man was hurting. Pain shadowed the strong angles of his face, despite his laughter. Suddenly, she felt incredibly guilty about continuing with her little act.

She drained the last half of her cup in practically one swallow. "I really have to be going. Riley?" The dog at her feet came to life and stood beside her chair.

"I'd like to see you again. Take you out to dinner tomorrow."

"Oh, you don't have to do that," she assured him quickly as she stood. "Coffee was payment enough for your little *faux pas*." Aside from the fact the rude jerk that plowed into her earlier had turned into a very intriguing man, she didn't want to see him again. He thought she was blind, and she already felt guilty. How would she ever be able to keep up the charade for an entire evening? Evening—meaning she wouldn't be able to hide behind her sunglasses.

"Please. I'd like to do this."

"It's really not necessary."

"Maybe not." He paused a moment, as if deciding whether or not to voice his next statement. "I'll level with you," he began, almost reluctantly. "You make me laugh. And to be honest, I could use a little laughter in my life."

Holly stared at him. It was painfully apparent he was telling the truth, and her heart went out to him. She always was a sucker for hard luck stories. "Okay," she answered, against her better judgment. "One dinner."

What could it hurt? They'd have one dinner together, then she'd never see him again. How long could it take to eat dinner anyway? One? Two? Three hours, tops? She could pretend to be blind for three more hours. After all, she played "Jill" in *Butterflies Are Free* in high school, didn't she?

She could do this. Piece of cake.

"You did *what*?"

Holly groaned and leaned her head on the desk in front of her. What had she been thinking? She was going to be wearing that cake, not eating it. "I know. It was a stupid thing to do."

Paige, Holly's best friend and co-worker, shook her head of short, blonde curls. "'Stupid' wasn't going to be my first choice. Hilarious, maybe, but not stupid." She laughed, patting her desktop as if it was a bongo. "You actually had him believing you were blind? What a riot!"

Lifting her head, Holly glared at her, even though the look was wasted on her blind friend. "What am I going to do? I can't go out to dinner with him tomorrow. I'll never be able to pull it off."

Paige waved off the protest with a flip of her manicured hand. "Sure you can. You train guide dogs for a living, for goodness sake. You had to live constantly blindfolded for two entire weeks during your apprenticeship, and you deal with blind people practically every day here at work. Hell, forget work. You've got me." She smiled brightly.

"Is that supposed to make me feel better? I mean, even if I can manage not to look at him like I'm really seeing him–"

"That cute, huh?"

"–how can I eat an entire meal in front of him? Okay, I know about the clock thing, but what if they serve peas and some roll off of my fork and scatter all over the table? Am I supposed to ignore that and pretend I don't notice? Because–"

"So don't order peas."

"–then he'll think I'm a slob...What did you say?"

"I said, don't order peas."

"No, before that."

"I asked if he was cute."

"You did not. You implied that I thought he was cute, and that's why I wouldn't be able to keep my eyes off of him."

"Is he?"

"What?"

"Cute?"

"That's beside the point."

"It is not; now tell me."

Holly sighed. She knew Paige wouldn't let go of the topic until she got an answer. "Is he cute?" She rolled the word around in her brain, then shook her head. "No, I wouldn't say he's cute. Cute's too tame...Cute's safe. This guy looks like the type who'd play chicken with a locomotive. He probably doesn't even know the meaning of the word safe."

"Interesting."

Holly flopped her head back onto the desk. "It's not interesting, it's scary," she said into the fake oak finish, then lifted her head again as a horrible thought suddenly occurred to her. "What if he's on to me, and he's waiting for me to mess up so he can expose me for the fraud I am? I don't think he misses much. Oh, jeez, what if he asks questions I don't have the answers to?"

"I doubt he's on to you, but either way, you won't mess up. Like I said, you've got me."

"You won't be there."

"Sure I will," Paige countered. "In a sense. If he starts asking questions, then give him answers. My life is your life," she stated dramatically. "See? Sometimes it comes in handy having a best friend who's blind, and not because I never tell you that your hair looks like crap."

"You do that anyway."

"Yeah, I do." Paige laughed. "And I bet you look in the mirror every time too."

CHAPTER TWO

Holly blotted her lips on a square of toilet paper and stared at the coral imprint. "I can't go through with this," she informed the two canines lying at her feet. Riley lifted his head, appearing mildly interested, but Bryton, her black and white Lhasa Apso rescue, didn't even blink.

"Dammit! Why didn't I get his number?" she admonished herself, wishing she could text him and chicken out. She took off the glasses she always wore when applying makeup, since she was farsighted, and laid them on the counter by the sink. Stepping over Bryton, she walked out of the bathroom and into her living/dining room. Of course, with as insistent as he was yesterday, Ashford Malone probably wouldn't accept a brush off text. "Maybe I can pretend I'm sick when—"

She hadn't even finished her thought before the doorbell rang. Adrenalin shot through her, causing her heart to race. Bryton barked furiously as he suddenly sprang to life and made a beeline past her to the front door. Riley merely walked into the room, sat down and waited.

Damn, he was already here. Unless she wanted to hide in

the back bedroom—and she refused to do that—she couldn't back out now.

"Just a minute," she called out, stalling for time to compose herself. When she'd waited as long as she could, she decided to stop postponing the inevitable and hurry up and get the evening over with.

She walked to the door, pausing with her hand on the doorknob as she remembered the way Paige always answered a door. "Who is it?"

"Ash Malone."

Holly steeled herself, fixed her gaze on the doorjamb, then opened the door. "Hi." She stepped back, still staring at the doorjamb. "Come on in."

When he did so, crossing through her line of vision, she caught a glimpse of the tan, camel hair blazer he wore and—was she wrong, or had he shaved off his beard?

"Bryton, be quiet," she scolded when the dog persisted in barking. Mercifully, he shut up as ordered. "That's Bryton," she informed him, still managing not to fully look at him. "He's a pain in the butt." The black and white ball of fur sprouted a tongue, panting proudly at his title. "You've already met Riley."

At the mention of his name, and since there was a new, unsuspecting victim in the house, Riley ran out of the room, only to return a few seconds later with a bright red ball in his mouth. He trotted over and dropped it at Ash's feet with a *thump-thump* landing on the carpet.

"Don't do it," Holly cautioned. "If you throw it for him once, he'll never leave you alone."

"I'll consider myself warned."

"Good. Why don't you sit down and make yourself comfortable? I have to feed the dogs, then we can go." For the briefest second when he was turning around, their gazes crossed.

Blue, she realized. His eyes are blue. Her favorite color.

Ash took her at her word and sat on the couch while she continued to the kitchen. Bryton followed her, once again proving his eerie talent for knowing exactly when food was going to hit his bowl, but Riley picked up his ball and took it over to Ash, an I'm-sure-you-meant-to-pick-this-up-but-forgot-to look in his big, brown eyes.

Since Ash couldn't see her from his perch on the couch, she was able to quickly fill the dogs' food bowls and put them in their respective spots on the floor. Bryton attacked his food like he hadn't eaten in a week, instead of just this morning. She made sure the water bowls were full and was washing her hands when she heard a *smack* followed by "good catch."

"Don't say I didn't warn you."

"I can't believe this is the same dog from yesterday. He's caught five throws in a row and keeps coming back for more. Yesterday he was so..."

"Serious?" she finished for him, leaning in the kitchen doorway. She managed a fleeting glance at his face before he looked up at her, and she focused on the far wall behind him. So he *had* shaved off his beard. Irrational as it was, she was flattered; even though it was impossible he would've shaven for her, since he thought she was blind.

"Exactly. What happened?"

"When his harness is on, he's a working dog," she explained. "A professional through and through. But when the harness comes off, he's free to be a plain old dog with the annoying habit of wanting you to throw his ball every five seconds." She smiled as the dog effortlessly caught another toss. "Come on, Riley," she coaxed. "Otherwise Bryton's going to eat all of your food before you even get to it."

Riley left his post at Ash's feet and trotted into the kitchen. After taking a deep breath, Holly walked back into the living room, running her hand along the wall as a guide. She picked up the shawl draped over the back of the recliner.

"I hope you don't mind if we leave Riley here." Initially, she'd planned on bringing him for the practice, but decided against it. The fewer people in the restaurant who thought she was blind, the better. Even though most people didn't do it to be rude, a guide dog always seemed to draw curious stares.

That in itself would've been fine, if she really was blind. It never bothered Paige. But since she was only faking it, the last thing she wanted was more eyes on her tonight. If she messed up and made a fool of herself, she'd prefer to only do it in front of one person. "I'll need to hold onto your elbow, if that's all right, and if you'd tell me when there are things like doors and stairs, I'd appreciate it."

"No problem." Ash rose to his feet and crossed to her side. Taking her hand in his, he rested it in the crook of his elbow. "I have to confess, I wasn't really sure your dog would fit in Jack's car anyway. Door," he declared, stopping in front of it.

Holly smiled, trying to ignore the urge to run her hand up the muscled length of his arm. Even with his blazer on, she couldn't help but notice the power beneath her fingertips. "Who's Jack?" she asked, a little breathlessly.

"He's a good friend."

"He must be to let you borrow his car with the possibility of an eighty pound dog climbing into it."

"He is. You left the bathroom light on. I'll get it." Disengaging her hand, Ash jogged toward the bathroom.

"That's okay." She suddenly missed his strength. "Just leave it."

"No problem." He stepped inside the bathroom to turn off the light switch. "It's all of ten feet away."

"Is that a crack about how small my house is?" she teased, knowing darn well that if her house topped seven-hundred square feet, she'd be amazed.

"Not unless you'd like it to be."

"Hey, now that was a definite crack."

"Have I told you how fantastic you look yet?" he asked, ignoring her last comment.

"No, but thank you. My friend, Paige, came over and did my makeup," she added for a touch of realism. After all, she always did Paige's makeup before any of her dates. Not that this was a date.

"Then those must be her glasses in the bathroom."

She nearly choked. "What?"

"There's a pair of tortoiseshell glasses on your bathroom counter."

"There are?" How stupid could she be, leaving her glasses right out in plain sight like that? "You're right," she agreed quickly. "She must've forgotten them. Good thing she doesn't need them to drive."

"Farsighted, is she?"

"Very."

Ash took her hand and once again placed it on his arm. "Shall we?"

Holly never would've imagined a man the size of Ashford Malone would be capable of being as gentle as he was with her. When he led her outside, he called out "step" for every one of the five steps leading down from her front door. She almost commented on the fact she would obviously know there were steps at her own house, but since he was being so sweet, she didn't.

He told her to watch her head when she got into Jack's

car, then proceeded to describe everything they passed on the way to the restaurant. He expertly led her to their table, pulled out her chair for her and personally handed her a wine glass before she asked, so she would know where it was.

Every nice thing he did made her feel worse about continuing to lie to him. Finally, after downing her first glass of wine, she decided to tell him the truth.

"Ash, there's something I—"

"Wanted to ask?" he interrupted. "If you must know, I borrowed Jack's car because I don't have one."

"No." She shook her head. "That's not...Wait. You don't have a car?" she asked, momentarily sidetracked.

"Nope."

"Why not?" She was amazed. She'd be lost without her car. "How do you get around?"

"Don't sound so shocked," he told her, then countered, "How do you get around without a car?"

The reality of the situation slapped her in the face, and she nearly gasped at the fact she'd forgotten what she was pretending to be. She cleared her throat. "I, um, walk mostly," she lied, knowing darn well she'd deliberately parked her car in the garage before Ash came over so he wouldn't see it. "Take the bus. That sort of thing."

"And you do fine. I, on the other hand, own a motorcycle."

"A motorcycle?" She should've known. Didn't she describe him to Paige as an unsafe type of guy? Of course he had a motorcycle. "What kind of motorcycle? A Kawasaki?"

"God, no. None of those foreign tinker toys for me. I only buy American. It's a Harley Davidson," he stated proudly. "I had to sit on a waiting list for two and a half years to get that baby."

"You're kidding. A two and a half year waiting list for a motorcycle?"

"Not any motorcycle," he corrected. "A Harley. And yes, since I wanted one of the new models, I had to order it thirty months in advance."

"Jeez, I can't even plan a week's worth of dinners, let alone pick out something I'd still like two and a half years from now."

He laughed. "If you want, I'll give you a ride on it sometime."

She smiled and said nothing. *I'll give you a ride on it sometime.* "Sometime" implied in the future, and there wasn't going to be any future for them. Not after he knew the truth... which she was going to tell him right now. "Ash?" she began tentatively.

He reached across the table and took her hand in his. "Thanks for coming tonight," he said softly, giving her hand a little squeeze. "I'm really enjoying myself. I wasn't aware of how much I needed this until now."

There it was again. That was the second time he'd referred to needing a little enjoyment in his life. What had happened to him?

"I imagine police work can get a little hairy at times," she ventured, playing on a hunch. She must've guessed right, because his face darkened instantly.

"You could say that." He looked down and released her hand. "Would you like some more wine?"

He's trying to change the subject, she thought, not falling for it. "Please."

He picked up the bottle, then reached across to fill her glass.

"So, tell me about it."

His hand jerked, splashing Merlot onto the white linen tablecloth. "About what?" he evaded in a low voice.

"Your job," she clarified, pretending not to have noticed the change in his tone. "I don't even know what department you're in."

Staring at a point beyond his left shoulder, through her peripheral vision Holly saw him squeeze his eyes tightly shut for a moment. Pain. It was etched in his face—from the worried wrinkles on his forehead to the tense clenching of his jaw. She suddenly felt like she was spying on something personal and in a way, since he thought she was blind, she was.

He opened his eyes then, and she realized she'd let her gaze stray to his face. She averted it back to his shoulder before he noticed.

"I used to be on the SWAT team," he confessed after a prolonged pause.

"Used to be?"

Ash closed his eyes again and shook his head once before reopening them. "Why don't I read you the menu?"

Obviously the conversation about his professional life was over as far as he was concerned. She decided to drop the topic, since he appeared to be so distraught when he'd been cheerful only moments before.

"That would be great. The waiter will probably be coming back for our order any minute now."

Holly resolved to confess she wasn't blind after dinner. Revealing it now would be too cruel, she rationalized. Unfortunately, she couldn't make herself believe telling him later was going to be any easier.

Ash knew he was staring, but he couldn't help himself. He'd never met a woman quite like Holly Richland, and it had nothing to do with the fact she was blind. As she lifted a bite of chocolate mousse to her lips, then proceeded to lick every speck of chocolate from her spoon, he suddenly realized what it was about her that fascinated him. She took pleasure in every aspect of life, no matter how small.

Whether it be talking about her job at the guide dog school, or eating her dessert, she always seemed to find the bright side of things. He envied that ability in her. Right now he'd give anything to be able to block out the dark aspects in his life. Unfortunately, since his last mistake had cost someone their life, he wasn't likely to forget it.

"Mmm." Holly's satisfied purr chased his murky thoughts away. He watched her eat the last spoonful of mousse. "This stuff is better than sex," she declared, then froze.

Ash couldn't help but smile when the faint dusting of freckles on the tops of her cheeks was rendered practically invisible by the color sweeping her face.

"Oh, jeez," she whimpered. "I can't believe I said that in front of you."

"Doesn't bother me," he assured her with a grin. "Though I can't say it paints your other dates in a very favorable light."

She looked at him then, directly at him, and for a second he had the eeriest feeling she could see him, before she buried her face in her hands.

"That's an expression I picked up from Paige," she explained after lifting her head. "Guess I'm going to have to quit hanging around her."

"But isn't she your best friend?"

"Doesn't matter. It's bad enough when she embarrasses me when we're together, but now she's managed to do it without even being in the room. That's not good."

He couldn't help himself. "You mean, worse than sex?"

She groaned and once again buried her face in her hands. "That's it. Now I'm never going to be able to see you again." She lifted her head. "I hope you're satisfied. You brought it on yourself."

Actually, he was incredibly satisfied. Her comment proved she *had* been thinking about seeing him again. He reached across the table and took her hand. "Don't punish me because of Paige. I'll be crushed if I can't see you again," he said and realized he meant it.

Holly bit her bottom lip and squeezed his hand. "Ash, there's something I've got to tell you. I..." Her words trailed off.

He couldn't fathom what she'd be about to say that would make her so nervous. "What, Holly?" he asked softly, trying to reassure her. "I'm listening."

She took a deep breath and closed her eyes, then exhaled slowly. "I'm not what you think I am."

"What do you mean?" He furrowed his brows. "Are you trying to tell me you're not beautiful and funny and refreshingly honest? Because I'm warning you right now, I'd have to disagree."

"No." The word came out as a plea. "I'm not..." She shook her head. "What I'm trying to say is..." Another pause. "My eyes are perfectly—"

"Holly," he interrupted, realizing where the conversation was going. "Do you think I care if you can see or not? I don't. Maybe when I was young and full of myself, I would've been disappointed you couldn't see how sexy I am," he teased, "but that's not important to me now. All I care about is how you make me feel, and you make me feel like maybe the world isn't such a terrible place. It can't be with people like you in it."

"Ash, please." She pulled her hand from his. "Don't say that. This is hard enough as it is."

He sat back in his chair and waited. Whatever it was she wanted to tell him was important. That much was obvious. The least he could do was let her say it without interrupting. "Okay," he said, a terrible sensation twisting in his gut. She was going to tell him she was serious about never wanting to see him again. What else could it be? "I'm all ears."

She bit her lip again, so hard this time that her teeth left an imprint when she finally let it go. "Okay...I do work at Guide Dogs of the Rockies. That's true." She clasped her hands together on the table, twining her fingers so tightly it must've hurt. "I am a trainer, like I said. But..." She paused and took a deep breath. "I'm not–"

"Ash!"

One simple word and all of Holly's courage scattered like leaves in a wind storm.

"I didn't know you were going to be here tonight."

Ash rolled his eyes. "Sure you didn't, Jack. That's why you didn't ask why I needed your car." He smiled at the brunette standing by Jack's side. "Hi, Elaine."

"Hi. Who's your friend?"

"It doesn't matter whether I asked you where you were going tonight or not–" Jack continued, despite the introductions going on without him.

"Holly Richland, Elaine and Jack Fallon."

"–you wouldn't tell me," Jack pointed out. His wife elbowed him in the side.

"You'll have to forgive my husband, Holly. He has no manners. It's a pleasure to meet you."

Elaine held out her hand, and since Holly hadn't been able to tell Ash she wasn't blind yet, she had no choice but to ignore the gesture. "Likewise," she responded, her hands still folded on the table.

Elaine shot Ash a puzzled glance, and he quickly informed her, "Holly's blind. But I'm sure if you told her you were holding out your hand, she'd be more than happy to shake it."

"Oh my." Elaine touched her fingers to her lips. "I didn't know."

Well, he's not exactly subtle, Holly thought, but she still applauded the fact he didn't pussyfoot his way around the subject like many people would have.

"It's all right, Elaine," she assured the woman, taking pity on her. "Most people don't realize I'm blind at first unless I have my guide dog with me." *Way to go. Might as well dig that hole a little deeper while you're at it.* "Mister Fallon." Holly extended her hand in the general direction of Jack, making sure not to get the angle exactly right.

Jack took the hand she offered, and she cupped her left hand around his as well, making it a double-handed hand-shake on her part. Working at the school, she'd learned that was common for blind people to do.

"Call me Jack," he corrected. "Now, I know Ash didn't tell me he was going out with anyone as pretty as you, or else I would've made sure to have shown up sooner. And if I'd known you were going to talk him into finally taking some interest in himself and shave off that horrible mess of a beard, I would've brought my camera."

Jack pulled back an empty chair from their table and motioned his wife toward it. After a swift nod from Ash, Elaine sat down. Jack then walked around and sat in the chair opposite her on Holly's left.

"How exactly did you know I'd come here, by the way?" Ash inquired, raising one eyebrow.

"Wasn't much of a guess. Everybody knows The Trade Wind is your favorite restaurant. Did he order the ribeye?" he asked Holly, then continued without waiting for a response. "Of course he did. Have to admit, though, it's nice to see you've got your appetite back. Elaine was worried about you."

"We both were," Elaine corrected.

"That's very nice, but not necessary."

"That's not what I heard." Jack picked up a bread stick from the basket next to Holly's plate and began drumming it on the table. "Fuzzy told me you went in and talked to Lethcowitz yesterday."

"Yeah, well Fuzzy should mind his own business," Ash snapped.

The change in his demeanor from friendly to defensive happened so suddenly that Holly couldn't stop a curious glance his way. Luckily, he was glaring at Jack and didn't notice.

"My God. It's true."

"Drop it, Jack," Ash warned in a deathly low voice.

"Dammit, Malone, you were going to cut out without even telling your partner, weren't you? That really sucks the big one, you—"

"I said, drop it!" Ash stood quickly, nearly toppling his chair in the process, drawing stares from the people seated at the neighboring tables.

Jack complied immediately.

"Come on, Holly," he said after a moment of strained silence. "We're leaving now." He reached into his pocket, pulled out a set of keys and tossed them onto the table. "Thanks for the use of your car. I won't need it any longer."

"Ash," Elaine pleaded softly.

Muttering, "Sorry, Elaine," he walked around the table to

Holly, helped her up, then led her out of the dining room. At the front of the restaurant, Ash paid for their meal and asked the maître d' to call them a cab.

"Why don't we walk for a while?" she suggested. With all of the negative energy coming from him at the moment, it wouldn't take long for it to build up enough to make a cab ride unbearable. He needed to let off a little steam and a walk outside in the cool night air could be just the ticket.

"Walk?" He sounded skeptical.

"Please. I'm so full I think I'll explode if I sit any longer. Besides, it's a beautiful night. We can catch a cab later."

He shrugged, and she knew he was giving in. "You heard the lady," he informed the maître d'. "Cancel that cab."

It only took a few minutes to retrieve her shawl from the coat check. As Ash wrapped it around her shoulders, Holly caught the faint scent of soap. No fancy aftershaves for this man, she thought and suddenly couldn't remember why she'd ever found them appealing in the first place.

Linking her arm through his, she let him lead her outside. The fresh air was a nice change from the aromas in the restaurant. Cooking food never smelled as good after you'd eaten as it did before.

"Where to?"

"Wherever."

They started walking and traveled a few blocks before either spoke again.

"This was a good idea. How come you know what I need before I do?"

She smiled, but didn't say anything.

"I want to apologize for that scene in the restaurant," he said after a short pause. "It definitely wasn't the perfect end to an evening."

"The evening's not over yet," she pointed out.

He stopped walking and turned to face her. "You're right."

When he dipped his head toward hers, it was the hardest thing she'd done in a long time, not rising up to meet his lips. It seemed like an eternity before his mouth finally settled on hers, but once their lips touched, their breath mingled, time stood still.

Once again, she was amazed by the gentleness this large man possessed. His lips caressed hers, softly at first, then more firmly when she parted her own. His tongue slowly outlined her mouth, occasionally skimming her teeth, but never venturing past them. Finally, when she couldn't stand it any longer, she reached a hand into his dark, wavy hair, pulled his mouth down solidly onto her own and thrust her tongue inside. He tasted like the peppermint candy he'd eaten while leaving the restaurant. Peppermint and heat seduced her senses.

Before she realized it was happening, Ash took control and deepened the kiss. She shivered when his tongue stroked hers and wrapped her free arm around the corded muscles of his neck. The movement pressed her breasts against the solid wall of his chest, and she moaned softly at the contact. Ash responded by drawing her body tightly against his own. She was enveloped by his warmth, his strength.

And even though she was standing in the middle of the sidewalk kissing a man she'd met barely twenty-four hours ago, a man she knew practically nothing about except for the fact he *used* to be on the SWAT team and didn't like talking about it, she'd never felt safer in her entire life.

A staccatoed honk of a car horn ended the moment, and Ash chuckled against her lips. "I feel like I'm in high school again," he confessed, "making out in plain view of anyone who happens to come along."

"It's dark, isn't it?" she asked, still trembling from their kiss.

"Except for the street lights."

"Are we standing directly under one?"

"No."

"Then kiss me again."

Ash's eyes crinkled slightly at the corners as a barely perceptible grin tugged up one side of lips. His mouth captured hers without hesitation this time, his tongue thrusting inside without preamble.

Holly had obviously kissed men before, but she'd never experienced anything quite like kissing Ash. Maybe it was the mix of boldness, coupled with tenderness that caught her attention. The sheer confidence and power emanating from him—leaving no doubt in her mind he could take her any time he wanted—that was intoxicating. Or maybe it was that incredibly magical thing he did with his tongue. Whatever it was, she could kiss him all night and never get tired of it.

When he tilted his head and deepened the kiss, hot images flashed unbidden in her mind...Ash pinning her against the building next to them, hiking up her dress and having his way with her right there on the street. A wave of heat washed over her, and she dug her nails into his shoulder.

He dragged his mouth from hers and began trailing kisses across her cheek, down her neck and back up, over her delicate ear lobe.

"Holly, what are you doing to me?"

His words and hot breath in her ear made her shiver, and a mewling sound escaped her lips. She swore she heard him growl before he pulled her in tighter and rocked his hips, his erection painfully evident.

God, he was driving her wild. Just kissing him was making her melt. How would she respond if he actually—

He dipped his tongue inside her ear, drawing a sharp gasp from her that sounded suspiciously like his name.

"What Holly?" he whispered.

She didn't answer him immediately. She needed time to compose herself, but her heated libido was making it incredibly hard to do so. She had to tell him. Things were quickly spiraling out of control, and she had to tell him before they went any further. She moved her hands down to his chest where she pushed firmly until he drew back. "I have to—"

"Shhh. You're right." He kissed her once more—softly, almost chastely this time—effectively scattering her courage nonetheless. "Maybe it's time we found that cab."

Holly spent the entire drive back to her house snuggled against Ash's chest in the back seat of the cab. What had she gotten herself into? Here she'd finally met a man who was intelligent, witty and who held her interest for more than the first five minutes, and he thought she was beautiful and funny...and *blind*. What a mess.

He deserved to know the truth. She had to tell him tonight. Continuing to lie to him was unnecessary and cruel. No matter how much she wanted to avoid that particular conversation, she knew she couldn't keep up the charade forever. She didn't even want to. Oh, she couldn't deny it had been fun watching him eat his own words at first, but that was before she knew him. That was before he kissed her. That was before she frantically counted off all of the reasons her mother said it was wrong to sleep with a man on the first date.

"You're so quiet," Ash commented as they climbed the steps to her front door.

"Am I?" The quiet before the storm, she thought miserably. How loudly would he slam the door on his way out after learning the truth?

"I had a wonderful time."

"Me too." If he remembered nothing else good about this evening, she wanted him to remember that. Turning to face him, she lifted up on tiptoes and kissed him tenderly. "I've never enjoyed myself more."

"It doesn't have to end here." He took her hand in his and stroked his thumb slowly back and forth across her skin.

I hope not, she prayed silently. Please, don't let it end here.

"Would you like to come in for a while?" she asked, realizing if she had to tell him the truth—and she did—then she'd rather say it when they were both sitting down. "I could make some coffee."

"I'd love to come in." His voice was low, suggestive, and she shivered in spite of her attempt not to.

Holly unlocked the front door and stepped inside, but before she could turn on the light, Ash swept her into his arms. With his mouth on hers, setting her senses ablaze, she was only vaguely aware of the fact he'd closed the door by backing them into it. He leaned against it and pulled her close.

"If I'm moving too fast, tell me." His lips were a breath above hers, his hands slowly tracing erotic patterns up and down her spine. She desperately tried to ignore the warm sensations evoked.

"Ash..." It's now or never, she realized. *Tell him!* "I don't really know how to say this, but—"

He silenced her confession with a kiss, tangling her guilt with want and need before asking, "Do you want to see me again?"

"Yes," she answered breathlessly, "but—"

"Then that's all I need to hear." He reclaimed her mouth with a kiss that made every kiss she'd ever experienced with other men seem insignificant. As insignificant as the one she'd shared in the closet with Bobby Grayson at a third grade party after the spinning bottle had stopped on them. "Sweet dreams, Holly."

Before she realized what was happening, Ash opened the door and was gone. Her nervous fingers fumbled with the doorknob, but by the time she managed to reopen it, he was nowhere in sight.

"Ash?" she called to the darkness.

Only the crickets answered her.

CHAPTER THREE

"So, did you ever get any sleep?"

Holly looked up from the coffee maker in the break room to find Paige and her guide dog, Charm, standing in the doorway. Obviously, she'd been unsuccessful in sneaking in to work without Paige hearing her. "Not much," she admitted, deciding to forgo her regular cream in the hopes it would make the caffeine enter her blood stream faster.

"Of course you didn't," Paige said. "If I know you, you were probably up most of the night worrying after we got off of the phone." She didn't say anything, so Paige continued. "Let me see if I've got this straight. Now, not only does this gorgeous hunk of male think you're blind, but he also thinks I'm not." She laughed while Holly groaned. "This is fun. I can't wait to meet him."

"You're not going to meet him. Ever. I probably won't even see him again."

"Yeah, right." Paige scoffed. "There's about as much chance of you not seeing him again as there is of Charm suddenly turning into a toy poodle."

Holly looked at the golden retriever in question before asking, "Why?"

"Why?" her friend echoed in disbelief. "Get real. Like you can honestly stand there and tell me you don't want to sleep with the guy."

"Paige!"

"I rest my case."

"This is ridiculous," Holly declared, mortified to realize she was blushing. She abandoned her coffee on the counter and pushed past Paige on her way through the doorway.

"Where're you going? The conversation's just getting good."

"The conversation's over," she said, walking toward the back door. "I don't have time for this. Riley's only got eleven days left."

"Where is the Rilster?"

"I left him out back."

"Didn't do you any good. I heard you anyway."

"Get a life," Holly ordered, stepping outside and closing the door behind her.

"I've got a life," Paige called. "But at the moment, yours is way more entertaining. We're talking Oscar material here!"

"Is that 'we' meaning you and the dog?"

Paige gasped and swung toward the voice. A rich, deep, sexy voice, she noted. "Who wants to know?"

"Ash Malone. I'm looking for one of your instructors… Holly Richland."

"No way!" Paige exclaimed before she could stop herself. He was the guy from last night. The one who thought Holly was blind and that she was−

"Excuse me?"

"No way," she repeated quickly. "No way I don't know Holly. Everybody here does."

"Great. Can you point me in the right direction?"

He's got a "melt me" voice, Paige decided. The kind of voice that makes you pant and drop your panties before you even realize what you're doing. "I'll do you one better," she told him, knowing she had to try to warn Holly. "I'll take you to her."

"Thanks. Miss...?"

"Tanner," Paige supplied, extending her hand. "Paige Tanner."

Ash shook her hand firmly. "Paige," he echoed, the recognition evident in his voice. "You're the friend Holly speaks so highly of."

Paige smiled directly at him...she hoped. "That's me."

"Pleasure to meet you."

"You too." What was she supposed to do now? If Holly was right outside instead of back in the kennels, and she walked right past her, it would blow everything. "Would you like some coffee?" she asked, stalling for time to decide how to best proceed.

"I'd kill for a cup."

Paige recognized him as a fellow caffeine addict and laughed. "Help yourself." She motioned to the break room. "I have to get something out of my office, then I'll take you to her." She waited until she heard him walk past and into the lounge before she gave Charm the command to head to the back door. Someone opened it before she reached it.

"I need my coffee."

"Shhh," Paige ordered, recognizing Holly's voice. "He's here."

"Who's here?"

"Holly?"

When Ashford Malone appeared in the hallway, Holly

nearly dropped dead from the shock. She grabbed Paige's arm like it was a lifeline and squeezed.

"I found her," Paige declared, stepping in and rescuing the situation. "Holly, guess who's here? Your friend, Ash. We were just coming to look for you."

Holly's heartbeat escalated as Ash started toward her, his long strides quickly eating up the short distance between them. As much as she couldn't afford to see him, especially here at the school, she couldn't deny she was glad he'd come.

"Hi." He reached out to touch her arm, like he wanted to let her know where he was standing.

"Ash. What a surprise." She tried to ignore the heat spilling into her veins where his hand brushed her skin. "What're you doing here?"

"When I woke up this morning, you were the first thing I thought of," he confessed. "Coffee was second, but I was out, so I got on my bike to get some. Before I knew it, I was here."

"Wow." It was Paige. She was probably enjoying this little disaster, gleaning every drop of information she could to confront her with later.

"Did Paige offer you some coffee, I hope?" she asked, ignoring the steaming cup in his hands.

"She did. In fact, she's been very helpful."

I'll bet. She was definitely going to have a little talk with Paige once he'd left about how easy the words "she's not here" would've been to say.

"Where's Riley?" he asked.

"Outside. I came back in to grab my coffee."

"Holly maneuvers around the inside of this place so well," Paige explained, "you'd swear she could see."

Holly swallowed the lump that suddenly appeared in her throat. She refrained from kicking Paige's foot, but made a mental note to move her stash of Twinkies from her desk drawer to the window sill in retaliation.

"Paige, don't you have some work to do?"

Her smile was so wide; she looked like the Cheshire cat. "Not until my appointment at nine-thirty."

"Better get ready," Holly said pointedly.

Paige rolled her eyes. "I suppose I could get ready for that." She turned toward Ash. "It was nice meeting you. Hopefully I'll see you around here again soon."

"Nice meeting you, as well."

"Charm, forward."

Ash watched her leave. "Is Paige a trainer too?"

"No, she's a counselor," Holly automatically responded before thinking, then quickly added, "Charm is still in training. She's spending a week with Paige so she can get used to sitting quietly in an office." That was a bald-faced lie—Charm and Paige had been a team for three years now—but she couldn't tell him that. "A lot of the people we place dogs with have nine to five jobs. The dogs have to behave properly in an office."

"Makes sense."

"Holly," Paige called from outside of her office doorway. "Don't forget your coffee again. It's in the lounge where you left it."

"Thanks," she responded, then addressed Ash. "Why don't you go on out back? You can keep Riley company. I'll just be a minute."

"Okay."

As soon as he was outside with the door closed behind him, Holly sprinted down the hallway and stuck her head inside Paige's office. "You are in *so* much trouble!"

"What?" she asked innocently, an individually wrapped Twinkie poised in her hands. "I thought I did good."

"No, Paige. 'Good' would've been telling him I'd called in sick or something, not offering him coffee."

"He surprised me. What was I supposed to do?" She tore open the cellophane wrapper. "Tell him you lied? I thought you wanted to tell him the truth yourself, but if you want, I can go outside right now and–"

"No, you're right. I'm sorry. This whole thing has got me so frazzled. I don't know my right side from my left."

"That's okay," her friend assured her. "Riley does. And speaking of Riley, don't you think you'd better get out there and take Mr. Velvet Voice off the grounds before Carmen shows up and blows everything?"

"Oh, jeez, I forgot about Carmen. She'd die if she knew what I was doing. Giving the school a bad name, don't you know?"

"I know. So get going. I'll tell Carmen you took Riley into town."

"Thanks, Paige. I owe you one."

"You owe me more than that," she said as Holly turned to go. "Hey, Holly."

"What?"

"Your hair's sticking up in the back."

"Oh, thanks." She absently touched a hand to her ponytail as she headed for the lounge.

Holly's frustrated groan reached Paige a moment later. She laughed smugly and bit into her Twinkie.

Ash was sitting on the second to last step outside, attempting to teach Riley how to shake hands when Holly joined him.

"You know," he began, "your dog may be a terrific guide,

but he doesn't fare too well in the normal dog tricks department."

"Trying to teach him to shake hands, are you?" she asked, and he was once again amazed by her perception. "I'm afraid that stuff takes a back seat to everything else he's learning. The thing is..."

Holly paused so long he found himself looking up at her to be sure she was still there. She was wearing dark glasses. The sun shone down on her cinnamon-colored hair, setting fire to the muted red highlights. If it wasn't for the fact her full lips were screwed into a frown, he could've stared at her all day and not cared if either of them spoke another word. As it was, however, she looked too worried for him not to comment.

"What's wrong?"

"I...haven't been exactly honest with you."

"What do you mean?"

She took a deep breath, then frowned some more before blurting, "Riley's not really my guide dog. In fact, he's still in training. Actually, I've never been partnered with a guide dog of my own. I'm always training other dogs."

"Oh." That was it? The way she'd forced the words out, as if she was afraid to say them, he'd expected her to tell him something awful, like *take a hike*.

"I know I should've told you sooner," she continued, "but I didn't know how to bring it up. I mean, you assumed he was mine, and I didn't say he wasn't. I even brought him home with me the other night, so you'd think he was mine. At first, I intentionally set out to fool you, but I can't do it any longer. It's not fair to you. But I swear, I'm not usually the type of person to lie–"

"Holly."

"–and I promise I'll never do it again, but I ended up

liking you when I never thought I would, and I panicked. I was afraid you wouldn't want to see me again, and—"

"Holly..."

"—I couldn't face that. Not then, and I don't really think I can now, but you deserve to know the truth. So, if you decide to walk away, I'll understand, and I really can't blame you, but I need to tell you anyway. You need to know I'm not—"

"Holly!" He shouted her name so forcefully that Riley flinched at his feet. Ash stood and climbed the few steps until he reached her on the landing. "You're rambling," he whispered, running a finger across her lips, trying to erase her frown.

"I know, but—"

"Shhh," he commanded, silencing her by pressing his index finger slightly into her mouth. When her tongue touched it softly, he nearly groaned out loud. "No buts." Before he realized what he was doing, he'd replaced his finger with his lips.

Holly desperately fought to resist the glorious emotions his kiss evoked. She'd been so close to telling him the truth before his mouth covered hers, nibbling her lips, stroking her tongue, demanding a response...No! She couldn't back down now. She had to tell him she wasn't blind, and she had to tell him before his powerful arms drew her any closer against his warmth, before his strong thigh pressed it's way any further between her own, before his insistent hands pulled her any tighter against his hips...

"Holly?"

"What?" she mouthed against his lips, hanging on to sanity by a single thread.

"I want to make love to you."

When the thread snapped, she didn't even care she was

falling. The deep rumble of the words he'd whispered against her ear turned her blood into molten lava. "Yes."

Ash kissed her again, quickly, fiercely, before asking, "Can we get out of here?"

"Yes," she responded, without even thinking of the consequences. The only thought in her mind was an image of the two of them naked.

"What about Riley?"

"I'll have Paige take care of him," she said, deciding as she spoke. She opened the door behind them, intending to tell Paige she'd owe her for the rest of her life if she'd put Riley back in the kennels, when she heard Carmen's voice.

More jarring than jumping into a cold water lake immediately after sitting in a hot tub, the sound of Carmen's simple question of "Where's Holly?" galvanized her into action. She quickly closed the door and spun around to face Ash.

"We have to get out of here." She tugged him along with her as she descended the stairs.

"My sentiments exactly, but my bike's out front."

Holly shook her head as she frantically grasped Riley's harness and leash and urged him forward. "We can't go that way. We'll have to take the van. You can drive a stick, can't you?"

"What? Yes, but—"

"Ash, please, work with me. My boss is in there, and if she finds me talking with you instead of working, she'll be pissed." Of course, she conveniently forgot to mention Carmen usually welcomed visitors and would only be angry when she found out what kind of a scam she was pulling.

"All right." He opened the side door of the van. "I don't want to get you into trouble."

Riley hopped up into the back of the van, and Holly scrambled in after him. Ash closed the door and walked

43

around to the driver's side. After securing Riley into the travel kennel, she climbed into the passenger seat and buckled herself in.

"Where to?" he asked from behind the wheel.

"Just drive," she commanded, using every ounce of strength in her not to look behind them to see if Carmen was there.

When the van drove past the building, she caught a glimpse of Carmen and Paige. She let out a sigh of relief at their narrow escape and laid her head back against the headrest.

They must've driven ten miles before Ash finally spoke. "I'm sorry about that. Never meant to get you in trouble."

"It's ok," she assured him. "If Carmen asks, I'll tell her I had a friend drive Riley and me into town for a run through since Paige had an appointment. Ever since she gave me that deadline, she knows I've been working overtime with him, so she'll buy it."

"What deadline?"

"She gave me two weeks to turn Riley into a guide of her standards, or he'll get career changed."

"Career changed?"

"It means he'll flunk out of the program and never be a working guide dog."

"I thought Riley already was a guide dog."

"He is," she said adamantly, and she truly believed it, "but he hasn't passed his final test yet. So, now we only have eleven days left to prove to Carmen he has the right stuff."

"Why doesn't she think that now?"

Holly pressed her lips tightly together a moment before answering. "She thinks he has a problem accepting responsibility."

Ash furrowed his brow and studied Riley in the rear view mirror. "Why?"

"Oh, because he scored a little on the low side in some of the related areas in his puppy tests." She removed her sunglasses to rub the bridge of her nose. "But that's not unusual. We've had dogs who scored worse than Riley turn out to be some of our best guides. And once when she was working him, Riley was having an off day and couldn't decide which way to go around an obstacle, so he stopped and wouldn't move."

"The dog has to decide that?" Ash was skeptical.

"Yes. A guide dog has to take responsibility for his partner's safety. He has to make educated decisions."

"Isn't that a lot to expect from a dog?"

"It is. That's why over 75% of our dogs who start training don't make it."

Ash wrinkled his brows and gave a slow whistle.

"A lot of times, a guide dog will be directly responsible for his partner's life. He has to be perfect when there's no room for mistakes."

"And this Carmen doesn't think Riley measures up?"

"Carmen's not sure. But I am."

"You've got a fighter in your corner, Riley," he told the dog. "I hope you appreciate her."

"He does," she said, a soft smile curving her lips.

Ash gazed at her a moment before turning his eyes back to the road. The affection she held for the German shepherd lying quietly in the kennel in the back of the van was painfully obvious. If Riley didn't graduate to guide dog status, he'd probably survive just fine as long as he found someone to toss his ball. Holly, on the other hand, he wasn't too sure would be able to handle it.

"So, should we take the old mutt out and put him through

his paces?" That wasn't the original question he intended to ask. His first one went more along the lines of, *When we get to my place, would you rather undress for me, or should I tear your clothes off?*

Unfortunately, Holly brought out those damned honorable instincts his father had accused him of having when he told him how proud he was his son was following in his footsteps. Standing in his dress uniform at graduation, Ash had been flattered by the praise. A month ago when he watched an eighteen-year-old girl bleed out, he couldn't believe there'd ever been honor in him in the first place.

"That'd be wonderful. You sure you wouldn't mind?"

Mind what? he almost asked, before remembering he was the one who'd suggested taking Riley out. "Not at all." Funny. He couldn't pinpoint when Holly's happiness had started coming before his own desires, but obviously, since they were going to be walking through the streets of Denver with a dog instead of making love until they dropped, it had.

"Thank you." The regret evident in her voice told him she understood what he—what they were giving up in lieu of this doggy test drive. "And Riley thanks you too, even though he'd like to point out he's a purebred German shepherd and definitely not a mutt."

"Sorry," Ash apologized with a smile. "I didn't know he was so sensitive. Don't guide dogs have a sense of humor?"

"Believe it or not, this one does. I swear he walks me through puddles on purpose. I don't think he does that to any of the other trainers."

"Not even Cruella DeCarmen?"

She smirked and shook her head. "Thankfully, no. I'd never hear the end of it if he did."

"Now I know why I've never seen a Dalmatian guide dog."

Holly nearly choked on a laugh. "She's not that bad. In fact, she's a great trainer and a wonderful fundraiser. GDR wouldn't make it without her. It's a nonprofit organization. We never charge people for placing them with a dog."

"And GDR stands for...?"

"Guide Dogs of the Rockies. GDR is easier."

"So where to?"

She shrugged. "I don't care. Pick a spot. Riley's probably bored with all our regular routes anyway; we've been over them so many times."

"Do you always train in Denver?" Ash took the next freeway exit. If he played his cards right, he could walk them right past his grandfather's house. The old man would love Holly.

"Initially we train at the school, but for the advanced dogs it's necessary for them to get some real city experience. Since the school's situated halfway between Denver and Colorado Springs, we can use both cities, yet still be based in a rural location. It's a win-win."

"How do you get to the school?" He knew she lived in Denver, because he'd been to her house.

"Paige and I usually car pool. Unless we've got a class going through. Then I sleep on the grounds to help out with the students. They have to stay at the school during their training."

"How long do they stay?"

She smiled at him.

"Sorry. I'll stop interrogating you."

"It's fine. I could talk about this all day. "

She put her hand on his arm, and his pulse jumped.

What the hell, Malone? She touched your arm, not your crotch.

47

"Typical stay is fourteen days," she continued, "but it can sometimes be longer, depending on the individual."

"Wow."

"That's not a long time when you consider the students have to learn to walk and function with four additional legs."

"I guess you're right. How often do you train a group of students? You probably don't have any time for a social life when they're there."

"Is that your way of saying you'd like to keep seeing me, or are you trying to figure out how long until you can use the class as an excuse to dump me?"

Ash reached across, placed his hand on her knee and ran it up the bare silk of her thigh until it rested just below the hem of her jean shorts. He smiled when he felt her shiver. "What do you think?"

"I think you've got too much sex appeal for my own good," she confessed in a hushed voice.

"Mmm, I like the sound of that." He splayed his fingers wide and when two of them managed to sneak underneath the material, she gasped softly.

Holly tried to ignore the feel of his calloused skin on her bare leg, but she couldn't. His hand was literally only inches from the apex of her thighs, and the mere thought started a slow melting inside her. She wanted to slide closer and spread her legs for him. Make him pull off the road and do things to him that would get them both arrested.

She'd had a few lovers throughout her life—four to be exact—but she'd never felt so passionate, so totally uninhibited with any of them as she did just thinking about being with Ash. Maybe she'd finally found her soul mate, if there was such a thing. Or maybe she was losing her mind.

He thinks you're blind, remember? What kind of an honest relationship starts with something like that?

Gritting her teeth in frustration, she sat as still as she could manage under his mesmerizing touch. She didn't want to encourage him, yet she wasn't strong enough to break the contact either. She couldn't—she wouldn't—sleep with him until he knew the truth. There was no way she could deceive him like that while sharing something so intimate. It went against every moral fiber of her being. She had to tell him the truth before their relationship went any further. She absolutely had to.

She spied on him from the corner of her eye, exhaling a sigh of relief when he moved his hand from her leg to rest it on the steering wheel. Her gaze traveled along the tanned strength of his forearms, over the solid curves and planes of his chest, down to the button fly of his 501 Levis.

Heat flushed her cheeks, and she looked away. She'd wait until she told him the truth, but she'd better tell him pretty damn soon.

CHAPTER FOUR

"We just passed Monte Hoffman's cigar shop. On the right is Mrs. Barnaby's coin operated laundry and about a block ahead on the left is the neighborhood eyesore."

"You sure know your way around this part of town," Holly marveled as they walked down the quiet street. "And is it just me, or do you also happen to personally know everyone who lives here? I swear you've said hello to at least a dozen people."

Ash laughed. "I don't know everyone, but definitely all the old timers. My grandfather lives two blocks north."

With Riley on her left and Ash on her right, she was happily sandwiched in between. "The way you're talking, you could be a local." She paused a moment as a thought occurred to her. "Do you live here?"

"No, but I spent half my childhood here. Pete used to babysit when my dad was on patrol."

"Pete's your grandfather?"

"Yes."

"What about your mother?"

"Don't really remember her. She was killed by a drunk driver when I was four."

That's why his grandfather babysat him so much. "I'm sorry."

"Yeah, it pretty much sucked."

Holly flinched at his nonchalant answer, but she'd bet a year's salary Ash wasn't as unaffected by his mother's death as he'd like her to believe.

"What about your father? Does he live around here, too?"

"Shot in the line of off-duty," he replied, the bitterness evident in his voice. He kicked a rock off the curb and watched it roll into the street as they walked by. "He was a cop, like Pete, and every night after he finished his shift, he'd go to this same tacky diner for a cup of coffee. I'd had the coffee there," he said as an aside. "It was rank. Personally, I think he had a thing going with one of the waitresses. Anyway, some punk came in and tried to rob the place. Dad tried to stop him, and the kid shot him."

"My God." She felt sick to her stomach, yet incredibly lucky at the same time. Lord knew she didn't get along very well with her own parents, but at least they were both alive and healthy. "Were you young when that happened?"

"Do you consider twenty-nine young?"

"To lose a parent, yes," she answered. "How old are you now?"

"Thirty-seven. I'm hoping you have an Oedipus complex."

"Oh, please," she scoffed. "I'm not that much younger than you. I'll be thirty-one in six months."

"See, I would've sworn you were younger. Guess that makes me a dirty old man. When's your birthday?"

"My name's Holly. I'll give you three guesses."

"Christmas?"

"Don't sound so shocked. Can I help it if my parents have absolutely no imagination? I'm lucky they didn't name me 'Tinsel' or 'Mistletoe.'"

"They can't be that bad."

"You haven't met my parents, so I'll forgive you that comment."

Ash laughed, and since her overprotective parents had indirectly managed to coax it from him, she was willing to forgive them all the humiliation they'd caused her when she'd started dating. Obviously, he hadn't been kidding when he'd mentioned needing laughter in his life.

Riley stopped at the curb and waited for her command before crossing the street. On the left she could see a boarded up old building that had been the victim of more than one vandal's spray can.

"Here's the neighborhood eyesore," Ash said when they reached it.

"What does it look like?" She winced inwardly as she hammered another nail into the coffin of lies she'd built for herself. Sometimes she almost managed to forget what she was pretending. It wasn't until she verbally backed up her own deceit that the gravity of the situation really hit home.

He paused a moment, his hand cupping his chin. "It looks like a three-story shoe box covered with graffiti and boarded windows."

Holly laughed. She couldn't have described it better herself. "Sounds pretty."

"It's sexy, all right. The classic architecture, the bold, dynamic color scheme...the secluded, wooden view."

She laughed again. "You've missed your calling. You should be writing travel brochures."

"Right. I'd be great at it...Come see Denver's worst

feature. It may not be the Ritz Carlton, but the condemned sign does add a nice touch."

"All I'm saying, is you should be happy to know you have something to fall back on if you ever decide to leave the police force."

He smiled politely, but his face suddenly clouded over. His reaction surprised her.

"Ash?" she asked tentatively. "Is something wrong?"

"Nothing's wrong."

She knew better. "It has something to do with your job, doesn't it? Your friend, Jack, mentioned it the other night, and you got upset then too."

"I'm not upset," he snapped. "I don't want to talk about it."

"It might make you feel better."

"It won't."

He turned and started walking, so Holly gave Riley the command and followed along behind him. He was staring at the ground as he walked, not paying any attention to his surroundings. To be truthful, neither was she. Instead, she was watching him, but when Riley halted abruptly, years of training turned to habit made her stop too.

She blinked and noticed that Riley had stopped at the edge of an alley, whereas Ash was already walking across. Sometimes working with a guide dog was so annoying. How was she supposed to catch up and talk to him if Riley kept stopping every five steps?

"Riley, forward," she commanded, but he ignored her. "Riley, forward," she repeated, but the dog wouldn't budge. Suddenly, the hair on her arms stood on end. The only time a guide dog was trained to disobey a direct order was when some sort of danger was involved.

Quickly scanning the area, she spotted a virtually soundless car speeding down the alley directly toward Ash. There wasn't time to shout a warning, only time to act. She dropped Riley's harness and leash and sprinted forward with all her might. She barreled into him with enough force to safely propel them both across the alley just as the careening car went whizzing by.

Ash tumbled to the sidewalk, and Holly followed, vaguely aware of Riley barking in the background as she hit the concrete. Her sunglasses smashed and fell off when she hit her head, but she and Ash had rolled two times before she even registered any pain.

When they finally stopped, she was lying on top of him, her legs straddling his.

"Ash, are you all right?" she cried frantically, staring down into his dazed blue eyes. "Are you okay?" She searched his face for any signs of blood or injuries, ignoring the fact her vision was blurred. "Ash, *say* something," she demanded when he still remained silent.

"You can see."

CHAPTER FIVE

A sh watched as the woman lying on top of him turned white as a ghost. A chill raked his body. "My God," he whispered, the bile rising in his throat. "You really *can* see."

"I can explain."

"Get off me," he ordered, hurt and betrayal coursing through his veins. The last thing he wanted now was to see those soft, sherry brown eyes of hers and know that they truly were seeing back.

"Ash, please…"

"Get off!" he repeated, grasping her shoulders and pushing her away, literally bench-pressing her up and off of his body until she put her feet down on the sidewalk and stumbled backward. He was standing before she regained her balance, but didn't make so much as the smallest attempt to help steady her.

"What the hell, Holly?" He winced slightly when he planted his hands on his hips, ignoring the bloody gash on his left elbow. "What kind of sick joke are you playing?"

The heel of her hand pressed to her temple, she took a step forward. He retreated a step.

"I'm not playing games," she assured him in a shaky voice. "I swear, I never meant for it to go this far."

"How far was it supposed to go? Were you going to tell me you could see before or after we had sex?"

She recoiled as if he'd struck her and swayed on her feet. Tears were spilling from her eyes when she finally looked up at him...*Looked* at him. My God, how could he have been so gullible? How could he not have known?

"Or maybe you weren't going to tell me at all," he concluded, practically shouting the accusation. He didn't care that they were drawing a crowd. He didn't care about much of anything right now except for making her feel as miserable as he did.

"How many times have you done this sort of thing?"

"Ash..."

"How many men have you seduced with your helpless blind girl act?"

"I didn't..." she sputtered. "You're not..." She wiped a hand down the side of her face, leaving a trail of blood in its wake.

Ash's gut constricted at the sight while she rambled on.

"I'm not seducing you," she insisted. "Like I could do...I wouldn't know...You're just being nice...I'm sorry. I didn't want to...You're just so..." Her words trailed off as she swiped at her tears, smearing blood across both her cheeks.

"Holly," he whispered. She wasn't making any sense. Something was wrong. For the first time he realized that although he hadn't been hurt, she might've been.

"I tried to tell you, but you wouldn't listen," she declared adamantly, then swung around in a circle, nearly losing her balance. "Where's Riley? He knows...Riley?" she called, bumping into a couple of people who'd come to stare. "Riley?"

"Holly, you should sit down." She was scaring him now. If Riley could be standing any closer to her than he already was, she'd be sitting on him.

"Stay away from me." She was holding her head again. "You hate me."

"I don't hate you," he assured her and realized he meant it. True, he'd like to wring her pretty little neck for lying to him, but that could wait until he was certain she was all right. "I'm actually pretty fond of you."

"No, you're not." She shook her head, then squeezed her eyes shut as pain washed over her features. She stumbled sideways.

Ash saw his opening and moved to gather her into his arms. She resisted at first, then her knees buckled, and she fell against him.

"Holly?"

He picked her up and when her head lolled onto his shoulder, he broke out in a cold sweat. Riley stood at his feet, whining softly.

"It's okay, boy," he told the dog. "She's gonna be all right. She has to be. I'm not through yelling at her yet."

"She's going to be fine."

Upon hearing the emergency room doctor's words, Ash let out the breath he hadn't been aware of holding.

"Miss Richland has a concussion, so she'll have to be awakened every two or three hours tonight to make sure she's coherent. It took twelve stitches to sew up the cut on her forehead, and she has a few scrapes and bruises, but she's fine otherwise."

"Thank God."

"Is there someone who can stay with her tonight?

"I will."

The doctor nodded. "The stitches will have to be removed in a week. Don't let her get them wet. She can come back here, or her regular physician can remove them, whichever she prefers."

"Thanks. How soon before she can get out of here?"

"I've given her some medication for the pain and to help her sleep, so she's a little groggy, but you can take her home whenever you like."

As if he understood, Riley thumped his big tail on the floor. The doctor leaned over and patted him on the head.

"I have to admit I'm a little curious as to why you have a Seeing Eye dog with you when neither one of you is blind."

Ash huffed out a breath before giving the easy answer. "Holly trains guide dogs."

"Well, he certainly is well-behaved. The doctor straightened and offered a smile. "Miss Richland is in room four." He motioned down the hall. "The medication I gave her should last most of the day, but if her head starts hurting, feel free to give her some Tylenol before bedtime tonight. Make sure she gets plenty of rest the next few days."

"Will do, Doc. Thanks."

Ash led Riley down the hallway to room four, the shepherd's toenails clicking on the vinyl tile, echoing softly in the narrow space.

Holly was lying on the bed, her eyes closed. She looked so angelic with her dark lashes resting lightly on the smooth creaminess of her cheeks. He reached out and lightly brushed a strand of hair off her forehead, away from the gauze covering her stitches.

"Hey, you," he whispered.

Her eyes opened slowly, incredibly bright compared to her pale face. "Hey, yourself."

"How are you feeling?"

"Like my head went through an orange juicer."

"Sounds fun."

Despite his attempt at lightness, her face grew serious. "I'm sorry." She barely whispered the words.

"For what? Saving my life? Which you did, by the way. Thank you."

"No, for—"

"Holly," he interrupted. He was still angry with her for lying to him, but now was not the time, nor the place to get into it. She was in no shape for an argument and that particular topic was bound to get explosive. "Let's talk about it later. Right now, Riley and I are going to take you home."

"Riley's here?"

"He sure is." Ash patted the bed with his hand, and the German shepherd stood on his hind legs to rest his front paws on the sheet.

She rolled over until she was nose to nose with the dog. "Hi, kiddo," she whispered, rubbing his ear. "Sorry I doubted you. I owe you one." Riley licked her nose.

"Come on," Ash said. "Let's get you home."

Holly was asleep in the passenger's seat by the time Ash drove the school's van up to her front yard. He debated waking her, but decided against it. If she stayed asleep, she wouldn't be able to argue with him when he told her he'd decided to take her to his apartment, rather than stay at her house. It would definitely be easier to care for her in a place familiar to him. Besides, even though she owned her own house, whereas he merely rented, his apartment was nearly twice the size.

Satisfied with his rationalization, he dug through her purse until he found her keys and told Riley to watch her until he got back. The instant he opened the front door of the house, a banshee went nuts inside.

"Hello, Bryton." He'd forgotten about the little hairball. "Remember me?"

Bryton answered him with a growl.

"Great. Well, Holly's spending the night at my house, so unless you want to stay here by yourself, you'd better be nice."

Ignoring the growling and occasional barks from the dog who sounded much bigger than he was, Ash walked into the kitchen. He found a bag of expensive dog food in a bottom cupboard and removed it along with a paper sack from a drawer. Leaving the dog food in the living room, he went into the bathroom and grabbed Holly's toothbrush. Next stop was the dresser in her bedroom.

He opened the top drawer first and was greeted by the scent of vanilla potpourri. He inhaled the soft fragrance, then nearly choked when he looked inside the drawer. He'd never seen so many lacy, silky things in one place in his entire life. Lifting a tiny scrap of satin, his mouth went dry when he recognized it for the thong underwear it was. He dropped the underwear on top of the toothbrush in the paper sack, but couldn't stop himself from inspecting the other flimsy garments.

He never dreamed that under Holly's all-American exterior beat the heart of a Victoria's Secret junkie, but he was pleasantly surprised and incredibly aroused by the discovery.

It was with great effort and a sigh of resignation that he finally closed the drawer.

The second drawer opened to nothing more exciting than some T-shirts and shorts. Uninterested, he picked up the top item of each stack and put them in the sack. Another drawer yielded a pair of socks, and he found a silk nightshirt and robe hanging on the inside of the closet door.

He took the paper sack and dog food out to the van first and then walked back in to get Bryton. He'd finally stopped barking, apparently having recognized him from the previous night, so Ash was able to pick him up without a struggle. Holding him with one hand, he locked the door with the other and walked back to the van.

He was grateful Holly remained asleep even though Bryton started whining when he saw her. He put the dog into the kennel in the back with Riley, then started the van and headed for his apartment as they conducted their doggie reunion.

Ash lived on the other end of town, so it was after three o'clock when he finally drove into the gated parking lot of his complex. Leaving the dogs in the van, he carried Holly up to his apartment and laid her on his bed. After he was certain she was settled, he locked the door and went back down to get the dogs and her things.

Riley initiated a quick bathroom break on the front lawn of the complex, to which Bryton wholeheartedly agreed. He made a mental note to come back down and clean up before the property manager got upset. She was going to be mad enough when she found out he had two dogs staying in his apartment, but it couldn't be helped.

Sure it could. You could've stayed at her place.

Ash opted to ignore that fact. He knew darn well why

he'd brought Holly to his apartment rather than staying at her house. This way she couldn't send him home—not that he would have gone anyway—and he'd be able to keep her in bed.

"Keep her in bed." He smiled. The idea sounded even better when spoken aloud. If it weren't for her concussion, he'd climb into that bed with her and make sure she stayed put.

~

"Holly, wake up."

The deep voice invaded her dreams, but Holly tried to block it out.

"Holly," the voice drawled again. "Wake up. I made you some soup. You should try to eat some."

Soup. Now that sounded good. Her stomach was awfully empty. She opened one eye, then the other. When Ash's face came into focus, she smiled. When he stuck two fingers in front of her nose, her smile vanished.

"How many fingers am I holding up?"

"What?"

"How many fingers do you see?"

She wrinkled her nose and swatted his hand away. "Two." She'd never been one to wake up cheerfully. "Keep them out of my face."

"What's your name?"

"My name?"

"Yes, your name."

She frowned. "Seriously?"

"Humor me."

"Holly." What a stupid question. Why wouldn't she know her own name?

Ash smiled and she almost wished he'd ask her more pointless questions so she could stare at him a little longer. Lord, but he was a handsome man. How had she ever thought him otherwise?

"How're you feeling?"

She sat up in the king-sized bed, wincing when the action made her head throb. "My head hurts," she said, remembering the accident. "Where am I?" She didn't recall hospitals having king-sized beds.

A bulletin board with a map of the city pinned to it was the sole ornamentation on the walls, and aside from the bed, a mismatched dresser and nightstand were the only other things in the room. This was the dreariest hospital she'd ever been in.

"I thought they said I could go home."

"You are home. Well, my home," he amended.

"We're at your house?" She finally noticed the pile of dirty clothes in the corner. Definitely not a hospital.

"Not exactly out of the pages of *Good Housekeeping,* is it?"

"Well..."

"I don't spend much time here, so just need the basics."

She nodded as if she understood perfectly when, in fact, she was pondering the question as to where he *did* spend his time. Did he have so many girlfriends he rotated through them every week?

"Why didn't you take me to my house?"

"Because I have to make sure you rest, like you're supposed to." His that's-the-way-it-is-so-deal-with-it tone revealed he obviously expected her to challenge him.

In all honesty, she was too tired and sore to argue. "I thought you hated me." Her voice was almost a whisper.

Ash's jaw clenched. "I don't hate you. Eat your soup."

Holly knew they'd have to talk about her deception sooner or later, but if he was willing to let it be later, she wasn't about to argue. That was one conversation she was definitely not looking forward to having, so she ate the soup instead.

It wasn't until she'd finished the bowl that she remembered the dogs. "Oh no. I left Bryton inside this morning. He was hiding under the bed and wouldn't come out, so I let him stay in. He's probably dying to go to the bathroom." She glanced at the clock on the nightstand to her left. It was a little after seven p.m. Poor little guy.

"Don't worry about him. He's fine."

He motioned to the floor. Lying next to Riley on the boring tan carpet, Bryton was sprawled on his back, his hind legs spread-eagled and his front legs tucked against his chest. She smiled. "That's his lust-puppy pose."

Ash raised a dark eyebrow.

She laughed at his worried expression, but wished she hadn't. She pressed a hand to her forehead, grimacing when she touched the gauze bandage covering her stitches.

"How's your head?"

"I'll live. Thanks for bringing the dogs."

"Don't mention it. I also called Paige and asked about the van. She said it wouldn't be a problem to keep it here tonight, as long as we get it back tomorrow."

Paige. Ash still thought Paige could see. She decided to confess that later when everything else hit the fan. What a fun conversation she had to look forward to.

"Thank you for everything you're doing," she said, stifling a yawn. "You're being incredibly nice to me under the circumstances."

"I'm waiting for you to regain your strength," Ash

informed her with a wry grin. "After you're feeling better and I lay into you, you'll wish you were sick again."

She smiled sleepily before closing her eyes. After a moment, her breathing deepened.

"Oh, Holly." Ash sighed and brushed a stray wisp of hair from her cheek. "It would be a lot easier to hate you if you weren't so damn cute."

He pulled the covers up to her shoulders and walked into the kitchen to make himself a quick dinner consisting of chili dogs and taco chips. Gourmet chef he was not. He fed the dogs and took them out again, cleaned up their mess, then went back inside.

Holly slept throughout the evening. Ash woke her up every few hours, like the doctor ordered, but didn't get much sleep himself. Something was bothering him, but he couldn't put his finger on it.

Channel surfing from one station to the next, he finally decided on a rerun of *Family Guy*. Surprisingly, however, he didn't pay it much attention.

"She's fine," he assured himself aloud. Bryton, who had apparently adopted him, looked up from his position on Ash's lap and panted contentedly. Riley was sleeping next to the bed, unwilling to leave Holly.

He's a good guide dog, Ash thought, absently scratching Bryton's neck. In fact, he owed Riley his life as much as Holly. According to her, Riley was the one who'd alerted her to car.

The car. That's what was bothering him. What was a car doing speeding down that alley anyway? It wasn't much of a shortcut considering the actual cross street was only fifty feet further. And why didn't the driver stop when he'd almost hit two people?

Ash decided to go down and question some people after Holly was feeling better to find out if they'd seen anything. Most likely it'd been a couple kids joyriding, but he was still too much of a cop to not follow up, regardless of the fact he'd resigned.

CHAPTER SIX

Holly awoke feeling as if someone was whipping up an omelet using her head as one of the eggs. In fact, her entire body ached, from her poor scrambled head to her scraped up legs. Even worse, the inside of her mouth tasted like cardboard.

Well, what do you expect? You haven't brushed your teeth since yesterday morning.

She sat up in bed, ignoring the protests of her sore body, momentarily surprised to find herself wearing her nightshirt until she remembered putting it on in the middle of night. If Ash brought it, hopefully he grabbed her toothbrush.

As if on cue, the bedroom door opened, and two dogs barreled into the room. Riley laid his head on the edge of the bed, but Bryton threw manners to the wind and promptly jumped on top of it—and her—in the process.

"Ow! Jeez, Bryton!" She petted each furry head while simultaneously trying to avoid two very wet tongues. "Hi, guys."

"I took the dogs for a walk. Didn't mean to wake you, but they had other plans."

The deep, masculine voice drew her gaze to the doorway. Ash, dressed in faded blue jeans and a t-shirt that clung to his broad chest, was casually leaning against the doorframe watching her.

"I was already awake," she said, tugging the covers up to her neck. She felt virtually naked under his unblinking stare.

"How're you feeling?"

Embarrassed. Awkward...*Turned on.* "Okay. My head still hurts."

"I'll get you some Tylenol, and we can talk."

Before she could respond, he ducked out of the room. She knew exactly what he wanted to talk about, and she wasn't looking forward to the conversation. She debated greeting him wearing nothing more than a smile when he returned, then making wild, uninhibited love to him until he swore he didn't care she'd pretended to be blind. She might've gone through with it too, if she hadn't swallowed.

"Cardboard." She grimaced. So much for her great seduction idea.

"What did you say?"

Her eyes cut to Ash standing in the doorway, a pathetic deer in the headlights expression painted all over her face. She quickly shrugged and shook her head, playing dumb.

He scrutinized her a moment, before crossing to the bed and offering her two Tylenol and a glass of water. She swallowed the pills, then took another drink of water and swished it around in her mouth before swallowing that too.

"That should help your headache."

She nodded.

"Think you can eat something?"

She nodded more vigorously. Bad idea, since her head felt like it was going to split open, but she was starving.

"Good. I'm not the world's best cook, but I do make a mean Eggo."

She grinned in response, a tight little smile pinned to her face. Ash narrowed his eyes, studying her. She raised her eyebrows in question.

After staring at her for a while longer, he finally stood. "I'll go pop the waffles in the toaster. The bathroom's to your left, but don't take a shower. The doctor said you can't get your stitches wet."

She nodded a third time.

He walked to the door. "I brought you a change of clothes. Your toothbrush should be in there too." With a grin, he closed the door behind him.

Holly groaned, rolled over and buried her face in the pillow.

"Ow." She lifted her head, gingerly touching the gauze with her fingers. She'd forgotten about the stitches, but even the pain didn't chase her embarrassment away. Ash obviously knew why she wouldn't talk when he got close. Morning breath should be outlawed.

Pushing Bryton out of the way, she got up, stepped around Riley and picked up the paper sack on the nightstand to inspect its contents. She pulled out her robe first. A red T-shirt was next, followed by a pair of lavender shorts. Cute combo. A pair of forest green socks rounded off the ensemble. Great. She was going to look like a bag lady.

The last thing she pulled out of the sack was her toothbrush with a wisp of satin dangling from it. Realizing what it was, she seriously contemplated committing suicide so she wouldn't have to face Ash again. *The thong underwear Paige had given her.*

She hated those things, and Paige knew it. They'd been a gag gift for her thirtieth birthday. Paige swore they drove

69

guys wild, but they just drove her crazy. She'd tried them on once, but never wore them again. Figures Ash would single those out of her entire underwear collection. They were the only pair of thong underwear she owned. And unfortunately, they were the only pair of clean underwear she had at the moment.

With a disgusted sigh, she wrapped the underwear inside of the rest of her clothes, put on her robe and headed for the bathroom.

Walking down the hall toward the kitchen twenty minutes later, Holly felt much better. Ash had left toothpaste on the bathroom sink, so her teeth were brushed. She'd made due with a sponge bath, since she couldn't take a shower.

Unfortunately, even though she felt better, she still looked awful. He hadn't packed her brush, and the comb she found in the bathroom drawer wouldn't go through her thick, tangled hair without force. She'd combed it out as best she could with her fingers, but since it tended to be oily, it still desperately needed to be washed. And as far as her clothes went, she looked like a walking advertisement for getting an eye exam.

She paused a moment before entering the kitchen to readjust the god-awful underwear. Now she knew what a couple of teeth with dental floss stuck between them felt like. Finally, after shifting her hips a few times, she stepped into the kitchen.

"Hi."

Ash turned around from pouring himself a cup of coffee and gave her a very deliberate once over. Starting at her green clad feet, his gaze traveled up her bare legs—they both had scrapes on them due to their tumble yesterday—to her lavender shorts, over her bright red T-shirt, past her make-up free face to rest on her stringy hair. She wanted to crawl into a hole and die.

"Cute outfit."

"You're the one who picked it out," she reminded him defensively. "What are you, colorblind?"

"Sorry. I wasn't paying much attention. I..." His words trailed off as his gaze dropped to her hips.

She froze in mid-shift. Color burned her cheeks.

"I made some coffee," he continued, once again looking into her eyes. "How do you take it?"

"With cream, please." Mortified, she hurried over to sit at the rectangular table. If she was sitting down, she rationalized; she wouldn't be able to squirm. Paige was going to pay for buying that stupid underwear.

Ash placed a cup of steaming coffee on the table in front of her along with a plate of Eggo waffles. "I already ate. Hope you don't mind."

Holly smiled and shook her head. Of course, she didn't mind. Why would she mind? Just because now she had to sit and eat while he scrutinized her every move? Why would she possibly mind that?

She buttered her waffles, poured syrup over them and took a bite. "So, is this a secret recipe or can I have it?" Totally lame question, but she couldn't stand the silence.

"Consider yourself lucky. My cooking won't win any ribbons."

"Mine either."

"We'd better order take-out for lunch then."

"You don't have to feed me lunch, Ash. Besides, I'll be home by then."

"No, you won't."

"Excuse me?"

"Doctor's orders," he explained. "You're supposed to take it easy and get some rest."

"I can rest at home."

"You can, but you won't."

"What's that supposed to mean?"

"It means you're staying here until I say otherwise."

"Oh, really?" The nerve of the guy! "And who appointed you God?"

"No one. The way I figure it, you owe me."

"I *owe* you?"

"Small price to pay for regaining your sight, don't you think?" He asked the question softly, simply, dropping the words like tiny, incendiary bombs.

The effect was devastating. A chill raked her body, and she was instantly light-headed and nauseous at the same time. "I guess I deserved that."

"Yep."

"Don't suppose you'd write it off as a misunderstanding and leave it at that?"

"Not likely."

Holly blinked back the tears suddenly burning her eyes. "Oh, Ash, I'm so sorry."

"Why?" He looked defeated. "Why'd you do it?"

She swallowed hard. "The truth?"

"Would be nice for a change."

She winced as his barb found its mark, but she was determined to tell him everything this time. "The truth is..." She paused when her voice wavered and took a deep breath before continuing. "The truth is, when you ran into me, I thought you were the biggest jerk to ever walk the earth. Here *you'd* run into *me* and knocked me on my butt, and then you started yelling."

She dropped her voice as low as it would go and mimicked, "What's the matter with you? Are you blind?" She shook her head. "What was I supposed to say to an attack like that?"

Ash didn't comment; merely kept watching her—like a vulture watching a dying rodent.

She sighed and averted her eyes. "I wanted to teach you a lesson. I wanted you to regret what you'd said."

"I did," he confessed. "I felt like a heel."

"Well, you acted like a heel."

"I tried to make up for it."

"I know."

"And you still didn't tell me."

"I know. I'm sorry. It was just...I didn't know how to. I mean, at first, when you were being a jerk, it was kind of fun making you suffer, but then you started being nice, and I started feeling guilty." She stabbed a piece of waffle with her fork and moved it back and forth through the puddle of syrup on her plate. "I tried to tell you. I really did. But you kept thinking I was trying to tell you something else, and then I'd lose my nerve."

Holly couldn't stop the tears silently slipping down her cheeks. "I'm sorry. What I did was unforgivable. I don't blame you if you never want to speak to me again." She sniffed loudly and smeared away her tears. "But you have to know one thing first. I may have been pretending to be blind, but I never pretended what I felt for you."

Ash was quiet for a long time. He could tell she was hurting, and one part of him wanted to gather her into her arms and tell her everything was okay. The other part, however, was scared to death of trusting her again. "How do I know everything else you told me wasn't a lie too?"

"I swear I never lied about anything else. I..." She

suddenly closed her eyes, pushing her eyebrows into a worried, upside-down "*V.*"

He watched her closely, holding his breath until she spoke again. It wouldn't take much more for her to lose his trust forever and deep down, he didn't want that to happen.

"There is one more thing," she whispered finally.

He was afraid to ask. "What?"

"Paige."

"What about her?"

"She *is* blind."

"Paige? But I met her, she—" He stopped abruptly. He'd spent three days believing Holly was blind. Why should it surprise him that a woman he'd only met once could fool him too? "She's a hell of an actress. You both are."

"I never asked Paige to do that, but unfortunately, sometimes what I want from her and what I get are two completely different things. She has a mind of her own, and she's super stubborn."

Ash silently watched her. In fact, he took unscrupulous delight in seeing her squirm. He'd asked for the truth, but now it was almost too much to handle.

"Ash?"

Silence.

"Ash?" Her tears were flowing freely again.

"I don't wanna talk, Holly."

Her breath caught on a sob. "Ash, please. We can work—"

"I said I don't want to talk." He knocked his chair back and walked over to the connecting living room to put distance between them. If he looked into those soft, golden brown eyes of hers another second, he knew he'd fold and crush her against his body until he'd kissed her tears away, and he couldn't allow that. Not now. Not until he'd had time to sort out his feelings.

He sat on the couch with a huff. He could hear her crying softly behind him, but steeled himself against it. When her chair squeaked across the linoleum, however, he threw an arm over the couch back and twisted around to look at her.

"Where do you think you're going?"

She stopped in mid-stride, sniffed and squared her shoulders. "Home."

"I already told you, you're not going anywhere." His voice left no doubt he intended to do anything necessary to make her stay.

She stood there for a charged moment, narrowing her eyes, studying his face, as if trying to gage whether or not to challenge him. He caught and held her gaze. *You shouldn't.*

She was the first to break eye contact. He watched her perfect breasts rise and fall with each measured breath. She was shaking slightly—no doubt from the frustration of realizing she wasn't going to win and hating every minute of it.

Then with a seething glare, she turned, stomped into the bedroom and slammed the door.

CHAPTER SEVEN

The clock on the nightstand read two-thirty. Holly had spent most of the day locked in the bedroom feeling sorry for herself. She was sick to death of both the room and her attitude. The only words Ash had spoken to her since this morning were, "You have to eat something," when he'd had Chinese take-out delivered. She tried to eat, but her stomach was so upset, she could barely manage more than a few bites.

She knew she cared for him, but never realized how deeply until this happened. His rejection wouldn't be affecting her this much if she hadn't lost at least a piece of her heart to him.

So that part's gone, she told herself. You can still live with the rest of it.

No matter how awful she felt, she had no intention of continuing to act like a spoiled, lovesick teenager locked away in her bedroom. He may have hurt her, but she didn't need to let him know how much.

Lifting her chin defiantly, she opened the bedroom door and walked into the kitchen. Ash was sitting at the table reading something on his tablet. He looked up when she approached, but said nothing.

Holly followed his lead and picked up a chair from the table without a word. She dragged it back into the bathroom and placed it in front of the sink. Digging a couple of towels out of the linen closet, she piled them on the edge of the sink and turned on the water. While it warmed up, she found a bottle of shampoo in the shower. She may not be able to get her stitches wet, but she'd be damned if she was going to go another minute with filthy hair.

The idea was simple: kneel on the chair, stick her head in the sink and wash her hair without getting her stitches wet. The reality, however, was that only a contortionist would be able to execute that "simple" task. She ended up kneeling on the chair with her arms resting on the sink, her head cocked to the left. So far, all she'd managed to do was get one side of her hair wet and most of the floor.

When she knocked the shampoo bottle off of the sink, she could have cried from the frustration. She was about to untangle herself and retrieve it, when Ash reached past her to pick it up. All he said was, "This apartment isn't zoned for a pool," before helping her off the chair, turning her around and sitting her back down. Too stunned to protest, she let him direct her. He propped the towels up and leaned her head back until her neck was resting on them and her head was over the sink.

She watched in amazement as Ash opened the shampoo bottle, squirted some into his palm and began washing her hair. His large fingers were gentle and soothing as he worked the shampoo into lather on her scalp. She wanted to keep her eyes open, was fascinated by what she was seeing, but somehow they ended up closed. It felt so good, having him massage her scalp, having him near her at all.

Of course, her pessimistic side warned, he could just be leading up to strangling you.

She didn't care. Even though her neck was starting to get a crick in it, she wouldn't have moved if her life depended on it.

Ash used a cup to rinse her hair, shielding her gauze-covered stitches from the water with his hand. When all of the soap was gone, he turned off the faucet and squeezed the water out of her hair. He helped her sit upright, turned the chair ninety degrees to stand behind her and used a fresh towel to rub her hair dry.

Leaning her head back against him, she moaned softly when he dropped the towel onto the wet floor and began massaging her shoulders and neck.

"I'm sorry," he whispered in a low voice, so low she wasn't sure she'd heard him correctly. *He* was apologizing to *her*?

When she opened her eyes and gave him a questioning look, he bent down and kissed her softly. His chin touched her nose as his lips caressed hers. Before long, he stepped around the chair, knelt beside her and kissed her in earnest. She parted her legs at his urging, and he moved between them, drawing her closer, kissing her more deeply.

His hands positioned her legs around his waist, and she obliged his unspoken request, crossing her ankles behind him. She whimpered deep down in her throat when he ground his hips against her. She could feel him hot and hard beneath his jeans. Her first instinct was to unbutton them, but when he stood, lifting her as he did so, she wrapped her arms around his neck instead. Before he was able to straighten completely, however, he slipped on the wet linoleum, nearly taking them both down.

Ash chuckled against her lips. "I don't think I want to try that again. How 'bout a little help?"

With a smile, she untangled herself and put her feet down...right into a puddle on the floor. She let out a squeal when she nearly slipped herself, but he somehow managed to keep them both upright. Together, their arms wrapped around each other, they "skated" to the door, laughing in relief when they finally reached the safety of the carpeted hallway.

"Now, where were we?" In one swift motion, he lifted her so that she was once again straddling his waist. Stepping over the dogs at his feet, he closed the bedroom door, locking the bewildered pooches outside.

After placing her in the middle of the bed, he lay on top of her and reclaimed her mouth with a searching kiss, bracing most of his weight on his arms. When he moved his hips against hers, her entire body flushed. She wanted him inside her so badly it hurt.

"How does your head feel?" he whispered between kisses, his voice husky and deep. "Does it feel all right?"

Reaching down between their bodies, she massaged him through his jeans. "How does this feel?" she countered in a sultry voice. "Does it feel all right?"

Ash growled and rolled over onto his back so she was sitting on top of him. "Trying to be cute, are you?" He reached up and pulled her T-shirt over her head. "There's a penalty for that where I come from."

"Oh, yeah?"

"Yeah." He grasped her hips firmly to pull her downward while thrusting upward, drawing a gasp from her lips. Smiling, he pushed her soft, cotton shorts all the way up her thighs until they couldn't go any farther. Then he moved both thumbs underneath the material from either side and began stroking her through her underwear.

Holly's moan was more of a purr. She closed her eyes and let her head fall back as he increased the movement of his thumbs, capitalizing on the friction caused by the satin barrier.

Hot. When did it get so hot in here? She was burning beneath his touch.

Ash removed a hand and pulled her down for a kiss. The action pressed her more firmly against his other hand, which never stopped moving. She gasped, and he accepted the invitation, thrusting his tongue inside, mimicking the motion of his thumb. He didn't stop kissing or fondling until her breathing turned to shallow pants.

She groaned in frustration when he rolled them over. She'd been so close.

"Don't worry," he assured her, as if reading her mind. He kissed the sensitive flesh between her breasts before adding, "I'm nowhere near through with you yet."

That promise made her tremble in anticipation.

He planted small kisses along her collarbone, then traced the top of her bra with his tongue. His teeth grazed her nipple through the silky material, sending a shiver zigzagging throughout her body before centering between her legs. The ache intensified as he kissed and licked his way down her stomach. When his hot breath fanned her navel, she moaned softly.

She eagerly lifted her hips for him when he hooked his fingers beneath the elastic waistband of her shorts. The half-groan, half-growl he emitted as he pushed her shorts past her feet surprised her. She wasn't touching him and didn't remember doing anything particularly sexy to merit it, so she shot him a questioning look. When his eyes met hers, they were smoldering.

"You're wearing that underwear." There was a wicked light glinting in his smoky blue eyes. "I love that underwear."

The *thong* underwear. She definitely owed Paige an apology. Or maybe, she amended as Ash urged her onto her stomach and began kissing his way down her back, she'd buy her a truckload of Twinkies.

He ran his tongue along her exposed flesh, and she sucked in a sharp breath. He continued the caress, following the "T" back of the thong with his seeking tongue, leaving a tingling trail in its wake.

"What are you doing?" she asked, confused when he suddenly slid off the bed.

Ash patted her bottom, rolled her onto her back, gripped behind her knees and pulled her to the edge of the bed as he knelt down. "What does it feel like?" he asked, kissing her inner thigh. He playfully nipped the skin, then kissed a trail upward. Her heart skipped a beat as a rush of heat enveloped her. Spreading her legs, he moved aside the thong, parted her folds with his thumbs and licked her.

Holly gasped and bucked on the bed in response. She clenched the blanket tightly in her fists and held on for dear life as his warm, clever tongue drove her to the brink.

She nearly punched her nails through the material when the tremors started. Like a geyser, the sensation continued to build until it could no longer be contained. It spilled over, rocking her body with wave after wave of excruciating pleasure.

When it was over, she lay quivering in the aftermath.

"You don't need these anymore," he told her, slipping off the thong.

She was perfectly content to let him do what he wanted with her, until it registered that he wasn't touching her any longer. An irrational surge of panic made her prop up on her elbows to verify he was still in the room.

She found him standing by the bed, smoothing on a condom.

"I would have done that," she said, crawling toward him on the bed.

Ash looked up, a devilish grin lending a rakish quality to his rugged features. "Next time, I'll let you."

Next time. She liked the sound of that.

"What are you smiling at?"

"You." She reached out and gripped him in her hand, drawing a low growl from deep in his throat. Squeezing a little tighter, she began moving her hand up and down his length.

"Careful, honey." He stopped her hand. "I have plans for that condom."

"You do?" She batted her lashes innocently.

"You better believe it." With one deft movement, he was on the mattress beside her, pushing her against the wall at the head of the bed.

"Oh!" She arched her back away from it. "The wall's cold!"

Taking advantage of her new position, Ash cupped her breasts and squeezed them softly, gradually moving his hands around to undo the back clasp of her bra. He smoothed it off of her shoulders.

"I'll warm you up." With that, he bent his head to her breasts, giving them the same care and attention he'd lavished upon a different part of her anatomy earlier.

Holly arched her back further. Tangling her fingers in his dark hair, she held him to her, clutching him to her breast as if she'd die without his mouth there. That's when he reminded her he was neglecting other areas.

"Mmm." She moved against his hand, drawing his fingers even deeper inside of her. "Oh, Ash..."

He lifted his head from her breast, and she shivered when the cool, early evening air hit her wet skin.

"Last time, I couldn't see you," he whispered in a voice thick with emotion. "This time I intend to watch you every second, starting with when I enter you."

She bit her lower lip. His gaze flicked to her mouth for a moment, before his eyes locked on hers. "I want to watch you come apart for me."

Oh god.

She didn't think it was possible to be any more aroused than she already was, but his words just proved her wrong.

"Look at me," he ordered, lifting her onto his lap.

She stared into his eyes, but when he guided her hips and entered her, slowly and steadily, pulling her down on top of him, she couldn't help it when her lids fluttered shut.

"Look at me."

Obediently, she opened her eyes to the blatant hunger in his, and her breath scattered. He smiled then—a seductive, possessive smile—and she was lost. Any part of her heart that didn't already belong to him committed traitorous mutiny the instant their eyes met.

Ash moved inside of her. Slowly at first, then gradually faster until their rhythm reached a frenetic pace. He thrust into her over and over, crushing her between the wall and his body. She wrapped her arms around his neck and met him stroke for stroke.

Never once did she take her eyes from his. It was as if she was compelled to look at him, unable to do otherwise. His eyes burned for her, melting her with their intensity, and when her inner tremors began, his eyes let her know he felt them too. It was enough to push her over the edge.

She cried out his name as he pressed his forehead to hers and watched her shatter from the glorious sensations they'd created. With a final thrust, he joined her in the tempest, keeping himself deeply inside of her until the last shock wave coursed through them, and they fell back onto the bed together, still intimately joined, still gazing into each other's eyes.

Holly sighed contentedly as she bent her head to kiss his chest. "I hope this means you've forgiven me."

"I'm not one to hold a grudge."

"Thank you. You don't know how much it means to me to hear you say that. I was afraid you'd never trust me again."

She pressed her lips to his, but feeling his unresponsiveness, slowly pulled back. "Ash?"

Their gazes only held for a moment before he looked away, but she still saw…He *didn't* trust her.

"I'd better get dressed if I'm going to get the van back to the school before it closes." He gently rolled her off of him and moved to sit on the edge of the bed.

A knot building in her stomach, she watched him rake his fingers through his hair before she tentatively touched his back. He stiffened slightly, then turned to quickly buss her on the cheek.

"I won't be long," he said, standing to pull on his clothes.

"I'll come with you."

"No."

Was it her imagination, or did he say that a little too quickly?

"You stay here and get some rest."

"I feel fine," she protested. She didn't want him to leave without her. They needed to talk this out. "Besides, I have to take Riley back."

"Holly, you're in no shape to be riding a motorcycle. I'll take Riley."

She'd forgotten his motorcycle was still at the school. "I'll drive my car back then. I need to get it anyway."

Ash flinched slightly, as if her words stung. "You shouldn't be driving either. Stay here. I'll be back before you know it." Without giving her a chance to argue, he left the bedroom, nearly tripping over the two dogs lying right next to the door in the hallway. "Come on, Riley."

Both dogs followed him. She could hear their toenails clicking on the kitchen linoleum. A few moments later, the front door opened and closed, punctuated by Bryton's plaintive howl. He didn't like being left behind. She knew exactly how he felt.

"Brytie," she called. "Come here."

Two seconds later, Bryton bounded into the bedroom, took a flying leap and landed on her lap on top of the sheet she'd wrapped around herself. He licked her arm and nuzzled close. She leaned over and hugged him, feeling somewhat comforted by his furry warmth.

"It's scary being left alone in an unfamiliar place, isn't it, boy?"

Holly had never been in love before, but she wasn't afraid of love. It was the way Ash had acted before he left that scared her to death.

CHAPTER EIGHT

Despite Ash's suggestion that she get some rest, Holly hadn't closed her eyes since he left. At first it was because she was thinking too much. He was still upset with her and deep down, she couldn't blame him. She was determined to make it up to him, but he had to come back before she could do that.

She glanced at the clock on the stove. It read eight-twenty five. Ash had left GDR over two hours ago. She knew, because Paige called her the instant he left. Apparently he'd dropped off Riley and the van, filled Carmen in on her health status and then ridden away on his bike. Nothing out of the ordinary, Paige had reported, except she said he did ask a few weird questions. Questions like was the school doing all right financially, and did they know of anyone who might have a problem with its success?

Holly didn't dwell much on his odd questions, only on the time. Even if he was mad at her, he still should've been back by now. She was beginning to worry something might've happened to him.

As if in answer to her prayers, the doorbell rang. He

must've forgotten his house keys. She practically sprinted to the front door and flung it open.

"Oh!" She barely managed not to throw herself into the arms of the FedEx guy. "I was expecting someone else," she explained sheepishly.

"It's ok, ma'am." The young man smiled at her. "I have a package for Ashford Malone. Is he here?"

She sighed heavily and shook her head. "No, he's not. I can sign for it, though, if you'd like."

"I'd appreciate that, ma'am." She took the stylus he offered and signed her name. "Richland," he read aloud. "Is that correct, ma'am?"

"Yes." She was amazed he could read it. Nothing ever looked legible to her on those electronic things.

He handed her a small box wrapped with brown paper. "Here you go, ma'am. Have a nice evening."

"Thank you. You as well."

She closed the door and absently shook the small package out of habit. Not a sound. Uninterested, she placed it on the kitchen table, then walked over and flopped herself down on the couch to wait.

Holly was asleep on the couch when Ash unlocked the front door. Bryton lifted his head from his perch behind her knees, but didn't make a sound. He put his keys and phone on the counter, took off his boots, then knelt on the floor beside her.

His chest tightened as he watched her sleep. Here he'd finally found a woman he could actually imagine himself sharing a life with, a woman he felt certain would never bore him—in or out of the bedroom—and even though he wanted to, he wasn't sure he could fully trust her. Sometimes life wasn't fair.

Holly shifted slightly and slowly opened her eyes.

"Hey."

She smiled. "Hey, yourself. Did you just get back?"

"Yeah." He brushed her hair out of her face, then continued to run his fingers through its silky length.

"What time is it?"

"Nine." He kissed her forehead. "Have you been sleeping the entire time?" Lord knew he hadn't let her get much rest this afternoon.

"No, I was—" She stopped abruptly and stared at his jawline.

Ash couldn't stop the grin tugging at the corners of his mouth. "Worried about me?" he supplied, an irrational wave of pleasure flowing through him at that thought.

She hesitantly nodded.

"I'm sorry. Didn't mean to make you worry. There were a few things I had to check on and time got away from me." He decided not to tell her he'd gone back to his grandfather's neighborhood to look around and ask a few questions. There was no need to alarm her. Besides, he hadn't found out anything anyway.

Everyone he talked to remembered Holly and him tumbling across the sidewalk, but not one person could give him a description of the car that almost ran them over. Wait. Take that back. Mrs. Jenkins said she thought it was some sort of a pretty blue color...or was it green? He hadn't even gotten past square one.

"I'll admit I was a little worried."

He kissed her softly as a reward for that admission, since it made him feel so good.

"Are you hungry? We could go out to dinner."

"As wonderful as that sounds, I'm afraid I'd be a little embarrassed."

"Of me?"

She shook her head, deliberately glancing down at her clothes. "Of me. I look like a reject Easter egg."

He laughed. "We could order a pizza."

"Sounds good to me," she agreed, flinging her long, shapely legs over the side of the couch as she quickly sat up. Apparently it was a bad mistake, because she groaned and laid her head in her hands.

"You okay?"

"Sat up too fast. It's weird. One minute I feel fine, then the next..."

"Stay put. I'll order the pizza." Ash stood and crossed to the kitchen where he'd left his phone. "What do you want on it?"

"Everything," she declared. "Except onions."

He dialed the number. No need to look up; he had it memorized the first month he moved in.

"And olives."

"What?"

"No olives," Holly repeated. "Or green peppers."

"Are you sure you don't want plain cheese?"

"No, a combination is fine." The phone was ringing. "I've just never been fond of mushrooms, but I can pick them off."

"Do you like pepperoni?" he asked as a woman answered the phone.

"I love pepperoni."

"I'd like one large pepperoni delivered please." He held the phone away from his face. "You want any breadsticks?" Holly shook her head. "No breadsticks...No, we're set on drinks." After giving his address, he hung up. "It'll be here in thirty minutes."

"You could've ordered a combination," she assured him. "If you call back right now, I'm sure they could change it."

"Pepperoni's easier."

"You sure?"

He gave her a sideward glance that confirmed he was.

"What's this?" he asked, picking up the small box from the kitchen table.

"Oh, the FedEx guy dropped that off."

Ash studied the package. There wasn't a return address, which was odd. Federal Express required a return address.

"Well, aren't you going to open it?"

Something was off. A quick glance confirmed Holly was still sitting on the couch where he'd left her. "Yeah," he commented absently. Maybe he was overreacting. Maybe the car incident yesterday had him on edge when it was really nothing. Still, he couldn't ignore the fact the hairs on the back of his neck were standing on end. He fixed his gaze on the package and walked across the kitchen to the counter by the sink, farther away from the living room and Holly. Slowly, he unwrapped the brown paper to reveal a plain, white box. He inspected all sides, but found nothing unusual, so opened the box and removed the top layer of cotton. That's when his heart stopped.

"What is it?" She stepped into the kitchen. "Is it something fun?"

Blood pooling on a cold, marble floor.

Ash shook off the image and lifted a fragile, gold chain from the box. A small, heart-shaped locket dangled from it. He didn't have to open it to know that inside there was a picture of a teenage girl and her boyfriend dressed for the prom. He'd sat at his desk staring at it for hours before he finally found the courage to call her parents.

"Stay where you are or the girl dies."

"No one's been hurt yet. Let the girl go, and−"

"Shut up!"

He squeezed his eyes shut, desperately trying to block out the voices, block out the memories.

"That's pretty," Holly commented. "Who would send you a woman's necklace?"

Just a few more seconds and he'd be able to get a clean shot without putting the hostage in jeopardy. Ash stood in the middle of the corridor, aiming his gun at a balding guy wearing a bad suit, who looked about as stable as a bottle of nitroglycerin teetering on the edge of a table.

"Shut up!" Bad Suit ordered, yanking the hysterical girl closer to his chest, effectively using her as a shield while he pressed the muzzle of his .38 revolver against her temple. "Get out of here!"

Ash shook his head slowly, never taking his gaze off of the man. "You know I can't do that," he began, inching a step closer. "Don't you watch TV? That's not how it works."

"Shut up!" the man repeated. "Stop moving. Do you think I'm stupid or something? I know you're trying to distract me, but it won't work. Get out of here! All of you! You just want to shoot me!"

Ash narrowed his eyes. He needed to calm the guy down and he needed to do it quickly, before someone got killed. Slowly, he raised his left hand and gave it a decisive wave. Every gun aiming to shoot holes through that awful suit withdrew in response. He knew they weren't any further than just out of sight, but he hoped that "Mr. Fashion Don't" wouldn't realize it. He was jumpy enough as it was, and Ash didn't want him harming the girl. Lord knew she couldn't be more than twenty.

"No one wants to shoot anybody. That's why I'm here. To make sure that no one gets shot.

"Put down your gun."

"What?"

"Put your gun down," the man hissed vehemently.

"You know I—"

"Put it down!" he yelled, simultaneously cocking his own gun. The girl screamed.

Ash clenched his teeth tightly, weighing his options. If he didn't put his gun down, the girl would die. If he did, they'd probably both die. Or maybe, if he just kept talking, he might be able to talk some sense into the guy. Maybe.

"Okay," Ash informed him loudly, effectively informing his team, as well. *"I'm putting my gun down and then we'll talk. Just you and me. No one else."* He laid his .9mm automatic on the polished marble floor, then carefully peeled his fingers back. *"See?"* he asked, straightening slowly and extending his empty hands, palms up. *"My gun's down. There are no more guns except yours. If you put that down, we can talk."*

"I don't want to talk."

"Sure you do," Ash countered, taking a tentative step forward. The guy drew his eyebrows together, but didn't go ballistic...that was a good sign. *"You want to talk about how you're going to get out of here alive while the place is surrounded. I can help you."* He wagered another small step.

The man shook his head, and Ash moved again without him noticing.

"No. You're lying."

"I'm not lying. You think I want to stay here all day? Believe me, the sooner you get out, the sooner I get out. But to do that, you have to let her go."

Ash inclined his head toward the girl. The man retreated a few steps, pulling her with him. *"No! It's a trap. You want to kill me!"*

"No one wants to kill you. See my gun?" Ash turned back slightly. He intended to reemphasize the fact his gun was on the floor, when something flashed in the corner of his eye. It was only a second before he recognized one of his team peeking out from around the corner, but a second was too late. He heard the man's panicked words, "they're trying to kill me," followed by a gunshot before he could even turn fully back around. "No!"

"Ash? Earth to Ash. You in there?"

He flinched as Holly's question dragged him back to the present. Placing the necklace on the kitchen counter, he fought back the urge to throw up. Over. This was supposed to be over. That's why he'd quit the force, so he wouldn't have to feel this way ever again.

"Ash, what's wrong? You look like you've just seen a ghost."

But it wasn't over. Even though the man in the bad suit had been shot by SWAT members just seconds after he killed that poor girl, the fact her necklace found its way to him proved the guy hadn't been working alone. A dead man couldn't FedEx a package.

"When was this delivered?"

"What?"

"What time was FedEx here?"

"I don't know. Around eight-thirty, I guess."

"Eight-thirty?" Ash rubbed the back of his neck and let out a short bark of a laugh. "FedEx doesn't deliver that late on Saturdays." He started pacing around the table. "What did the guy look like?"

Holly watched him in stunned silence. Seeing that necklace had obviously shaken him up, but she couldn't fathom why. Maybe it belonged to an old girlfriend. Maybe he'd given it to her, and she was just now returning it. Or maybe, a horrible thought entered her mind, she wasn't an *old* girl-friend at all.

"Dammit, Holly! What'd he look like?"

She jumped at his sharp words and looked up at him. He'd stopped pacing and was staring down at her with wide, almost crazed eyes. "I don't know. Young, I guess. I don't really remember."

"You can't remember? Christ, it's only been thirty minutes!"

"Stop yelling at me!" she shouted back. "I'm sorry, but I really wasn't paying attention to the FedEx guy. I was too busy worrying about you!"

Her words must have sunk in, because he abruptly fell silent. He looked at the necklace, looked at her, then shut his eyes. She could see his teeth were clenched by the telltale twitching of the muscles along his jawline.

"Ash, what is it? Tell me what's the matter."

He shook his head, but didn't offer any explanations. "The pizza will be here anytime. I'm gonna wash up." With that, he turned around and started walking. He didn't stop until he was in the bathroom with the door closed behind him.

Holly stared down the hall, amazed by what she'd just seen. It was almost a minute before she turned her attention back to the necklace on the table. She lifted it carefully, watching the way the locket caught the light as it slowly twirled back and forth.

After glancing down the hall, she opened the locket. A pretty, young girl wearing a pink corsage and a tuxedo-clad young man smiled back at her. Holly didn't know who they were, but one thing was certain, the girl was not one of Ash's old girlfriends. She looked about seventeen or eighteen.

Why would someone send this locket to him? Or perhaps a better question was why would he be so affected by it?

She didn't have time to contemplate any answers, because the doorbell rang. Bryton started barking, so she picked him up and headed for the door. She was about to answer when Ash flung open the bathroom door. It slammed against the wall with a loud bang.

"Don't open it!" he ordered, crossing the hall to the bedroom.

"It's just the pizza. Do you want to eat or not?"

He emerged from the bedroom carrying a gun.

"What're you doing?" He marched past her without a word. "Ash?"

Holly couldn't believe her eyes. He was holding a gun, preparing to shoot the pizza delivery guy. He must be losing his mind.

"Who is it?"

"Pizza Hut."

Ash looked through the peephole before slowly opening the door. "Is that our sausage and mushroom?"

"No, sir. It's a pepperoni."

"That's right," he said, stuffing the gun into the back of his jeans before stepping completely out from behind the door. "We did decide on pepperoni, didn't we, sweetheart?"

He pulled a fifty out of his pocket. "Keep the change."

"Wow! Thanks. Do you want any Parmesan cheese or crushed red peppers?"

Ash looked at Holly; she shook her head.

"We're set."

"Okay. Enjoy your pizza."

"Thanks," he muttered, closing the door.

"What in heaven's name is going on here?"

"What do you mean?" He moved past her, dropped the pizza on the table and retrieved some paper plates from atop the microwave.

"Don't play dumb with me. You know exactly what I mean. You were ready to blow that kid away."

"Stop exaggerating."

"Ash." She hoped her tone told him she wasn't going to put up with any throwaway answers.

He was quiet for a long time before he spoke again. "It's complicated."

"Try me. I know it has something to do with this necklace. Do you know the girl in the picture?"

"No." His voice was low, barely audible. "I never got the chance."

"What's going on?" She placed her hand on his arm as he set the plates down. "Talk to me. You can trust me."

He shook his head softly. The movement was barely perceptible, but Holly saw it. The confirmation made her heart sink. He didn't trust her. Reality punched her in the gut, making it hard to breathe. She thought he'd forgiven her, but apparently he hadn't. How stupid could she be?

"You know..." She cleared her throat. "I feel much better. You should take me home."

"No," he whispered.

"I think we—"

"Holly..." Before she realized what was happening, he wrapped his arms around her and gathered her close. "I don't want you to go home."

A tear slipped down her cheek. "Ash, I'm so confused. I don't know what's going on."

"I know." He kissed her softly on the lips.

"This morning you hated me, and then this afternoon you made love to me..." He kissed her nose and forehead, waiting for her to continue. "I don't know what we're doing. I know you don't trust me, and I can't really blame you, but..." Her words trailed off into a defeated sigh. She tucked her chin and stared at the floor.

"Holly, look at me."

She shook her head.

"Please look at me."

Slowly, she obliged. Her eyes were soulful, glistening with unshed tears.

"I'm going to be honest with you. After what's happened these past few days, I'd be lying if I said I completely trusted you." She tried to turn away, but he held her chin, forcing her to look at him. "But I care for you," he said, staring deeply into her eyes. "I truly care for you."

He kissed her then, softly, tenderly. When their lips parted, she offered him a tremulous smile. "I care for you too," she confessed. "And as long as we care for each other, there's still hope. I'll earn your trust. I will. Please, just give me the chance."

"I'll try, Holly. Swear to God, I'll try."

"Thank you," she whispered between kisses. "I won't let you down."

When he returned her kiss and eventually deepened it, Holly figured they'd reached a truce. He didn't trust her, but at least he was being honest and was willing to give her a chance to redeem herself. Anyone who knew her would attest to the fact she didn't give up easily, and she wasn't about to start now. She'd make Ash trust her, no matter how long it took.

CHAPTER NINE

"He doesn't trust me." Holly ran her fingers over Paige's ivory brocade couch throw pillow. She'd gone over to her friend's when Ash dropped her and Bryton off at her house three days after the accident. Well, right after she talked herself out of burning those lavender shorts, that is.

She undid the fringed border of the throw pillow she'd braided moments earlier and started over.

"Well, jeez, what do you expect?" Paige plopped down on the couch next to her and started munching from a bag of nacho cheese Doritos. "It's not like you told a little white lie about your age, you know. You pretended to be blind. The guy would have to be a saint if he completely trusted you." She bit into a Dorito and gestured with the uneaten portion to emphasize her next statement. "In fact, I wouldn't trust him if he did trust you."

Holly tossed the pillow aside. "Gee, thanks for your support. Remind me never to come here if I'm contemplating suicide. You'd probably talk me into it."

Paige laughed. "All I'm saying is give the guy a break. He probably needs a little time to mull things over."

"Maybe you're right." She reached into the bag of chips and brought out a huge handful. Charm was a terrific port-a-vac, so she didn't worry when a few fell onto the carpet. "I just hate—"

"Not being in control of the situation," Paige finished for her.

Holly wrinkled her nose. "That's not what I was going to say. I was going to say I hate not knowing where I stand."

"What's there not to know?" Paige countered. "You have incredible sex together, and the guy's crazy about you."

"Yeah, right."

"Oh, please. He's been playing nursemaid for the last three days. You said yourself it was virtually impossible to get him to drive you to the school today to pick up your car, so don't try to tell me he doesn't like you."

Holly crunched into another chip. Paige was right. It was obvious Ash liked her. But "like" wasn't what she wanted from him. She was hoping for something more along the lines of trust...love...

"Don't expect too much too soon," Paige warned, as if reading her mind. "He cares for you. That's a pretty good starting point."

"How do you know he cares?"

"Well, let's see..." Paige licked the cheesy orange seasoning off her fingers before answering. "There's that small, minor clue of him—*hel-lo!*—telling you."

Holly laughed in spite of herself. "I'm worrying too much, aren't I?"

"You?" Paige feigned shock, placing a hand to her chest. "Worry?"

Holly rolled her eyes and snagged one more handful of Doritos before rising from the couch. She was careful not to touch the light material as she did so, since her own fingers were as orange as Paige's. Why her friend had insisted on purchasing a dirt-magnet ivory couch—especially when she couldn't see it—she'd never understand.

"I've gotta go. Ash is coming by at five, and I'd like to be able to take a bath." Her stitches didn't come out for another four days, so a shower was out.

She reached down to pat the golden retriever next to the couch on the head. "Bye, Charm."

Charm thumped her big, feathered tail on the carpet in response.

"See you tomorrow."

"You're coming in to work?"

"Don't sound so shocked. You know Riley's on a deadline."

"I know, I just thought—"

"That Ash would be spending the night," Holly finished for her. "Just because we've slept together doesn't mean we have to every night. I mean, yes, Ash is great in bed, but I want him to trust me out of the covers too."

"So he's not going to spend the night?"

Paige sounded skeptical. Maybe that's why Holly was so adamant in answering, "No."

"I'll believe it when I see it."

"Oh, now that's a real strong statement coming from a blind person."

"Say whatever you like, but you know as well as I do Ash will be the first thing you see tomorrow morning."

Holly denied the assumption with a decisive shake of her head, which Paige obviously anticipated.

"He will too."

"No, he won't."

"Will."

"Won't."

"Will."

≈

"Won't you consider spending the night?" Holly asked in a breathy voice when Ash's lips left hers. She was lying on top of his reclined body on her living room couch, waiting for his answer as calmly as a firing squad target.

They'd started watching a movie on Netflix, then got...sidetracked. She honestly had no clue when it ended or what it was even about, but was completely alert to every movement Ash made.

When his blue eyes darkened and he ran his hand suggestively over her buttocks, she shivered and burrowed against him. The heady scent of soap mingled with male tickled her nostrils, seducing her senses.

"Try to get rid of me," he whispered before reclaiming her mouth with a fierce kiss.

≈

All morning long Holly had to endure Paige's smug "I told you so" at work. The virtual chanting would've been enough to drive her crazy, if she hadn't been in such a fabulous mood. Paige could say what she wanted. Waking up next to Ash was worth it.

Even so, she could've done without Paige phoning her three different times last night. Calling and then immediately hanging up when she answered was pretty childish, even for Paige.

"You could've at least said 'hello' before you hung up on me," Holly scolded. "I would've told you Ash was there if you wanted to know so badly."

Seated at the break room table, Paige wrinkled her nose. "What're you talking about? I didn't call you last night."

"Sure."

"Honestly, I didn't."

"Don't worry, I believe you." *And Riley speaks German.*

Paige melodramatically placed a hand over her heart. "I can't believe you doubt me."

Holly merely laughed before exiting with her cup of coffee and walking to the kennels. She put Riley's harness on and loaded him into the back of her Ford Taurus, since Carmen had taken the van.

Counting today, she only had eight days left to work with him. It wasn't very much time, especially considering the fact they'd missed their regular training runs the last three days due to the accident.

She sighed and steered the Taurus along the gravel drive that circled the school. Reaching the main road, she turned right. She hadn't worked Riley in Colorado Springs lately. Maybe he needed a change of scenery.

"Malone? Did hell freeze over?"

Pacing around his living room, Ash clenched his jaw and sighed heavily. He should've expected a reaction like that. Jack was obviously annoyed he hadn't returned any of his multiple calls. "Cut the melodrama, would you, Jack? I need you to check something on the computer for me."

"Check something on the *station's* computer? I don't know. You don't work here anymore, and I really don't think it's ethical for you to have access to confidential police files."

Christ, Jack sure was milking this. He was enjoying

himself far too much. If it weren't so damned important, Ash would hang up on him.

"When did being ethical become synonymous with being an ass? Come on, I'm serious. I need a favor."

"Yeah? Well, I need a partner. Guess we're both pretty much screwed."

"Dammit, Jack." He kicked a magazine lying on the floor across the room in an effort to refrain from shouting. "I don't have time for this crap."

"And I do?"

Ash stopped pacing and shut his eyes against the headache that was doing its level best to pound through his skull. The power of speech eluded him.

After a good minute, Jack finally broke the silence.

"Whadda you wanna know?" His voice was low, almost as if he'd sensed Ash's inner turmoil.

"Did David or Beth Lyons report a recent robbery?"

"David and Beth Lyons? Aren't they—"

"Yes." He'd never forget those names. They belonged to the parents of the dead girl pictured in the locket.

"Hang on."

A muffled silence echoed across the line when Jack hit the hold button. Ash couldn't stop himself from crossing the room to the kitchen where the plain white box still lay. Carefully, as if it was a fragile life, he lifted the locket and stared at it. Heat pricked behind his eyelids.

"What are you, psychic?"

Jack's sudden words startled him out of the past.

"The Lyons' place was hit five days ago. No suspects so far. Looks like they took a silver tea service, some antique music boxes and a ton of jewelry."

"Did they list the jewelry?"

"Yeah...a pair of half karat diamond earrings, a silver

watch, a nineteen inch gold herringbone necklace, a gold heart locket, two...Hey, wasn't their daughter wearing—"

"Yeah. I owe you one."

Ash hung up the phone while Jack was still talking. So his hunch was right. Whoever sent him Gina Lyon's necklace stole it from her parents.

The phone rang.

"What happened to your manners, Malone? I did you a favor and—"

"I appreciate it, Jack. I do." He hung up again.

Two seconds later, the phone rang again.

"Jack, give it a rest."

He was just about to hang up a third time, when he noticed Jack wasn't arguing. He lifted the phone back to his ear.

"Jack?"

No answer.

"Jack, you there?"

Whoever was on the other end of the line hung up without saying anything. Definitely not Jack's style; he loved getting in the last word. Suddenly, Ash's headache came back in full force. Only this time, it was joined by an uneasy queasiness in the pit of his stomach.

When Holly arrived home after work that night she found a note on her front door.

Sorry I missed you.

She smiled and hugged the piece of paper to her soggy chest. Suddenly, the horrible day she and Riley had spent in Colorado Springs didn't bother her any longer. Who cared that it had started raining when they were six blocks from the car, and she hadn't thought to bring an umbrella? So what if some guy dented her fender on the way home, because he was too stupid to know a red light meant stop?

Ash missed her. Everything else was unimportant.

She unlocked the door and went into the house, kicked off her wet shoes and dropped her purse on the coffee table. Bryton was trotting around her like he was performing the Mexican hat dance and she was the hat.

"Hi, Brytie. Did you miss me?"

After two more circles, Bryton jumped against her shins and barked enthusiastically.

"I missed you too." She reached down and patted him on the head. "But right now I've got to get out of these clothes."

She was down to her bra and panties when the phone rang. Dropping the saturated T-shirt she'd taken off into the bathtub, she grabbed a towel on the way out. She wrapped it around her chilled body before digging the phone out of her purse.

"Hello?"

"Hey, it's me."

Just hearing Ash's voice made her feel warmer.

"How was work?"

"Don't ask."

He laughed. "That bad, huh?"

"Let's just say I would've rather stayed home and been here when you came by."

"What do you mean?"

"I got your note."

"What note?"

Holly hesitated a moment before answering, "The one you left on my door."

"What're you talking about? I didn't leave a note."

"You didn't?"

"No."

"Well, that's weird." She walked around the coffee table and sat on the couch. "I wonder who left it."

"What did it say?"

"'Sorry I missed you.'"

"Was it Paige?"

Bryton came over and sat on Holly's feet. Since her toes were freezing, she welcomed his usually annoying habit. "No way. I've seen Paige's handwriting. She says she used to have excellent penmanship before she went blind, but take it from me, its gone way downhill in the fifteen years since."

"I forget Paige is blind."

Holly winced at his words. It was easier to pretend she'd never lied to him, but his comment ruthlessly reminded her she had.

"It was probably one of my other friends." And even if it wasn't, she didn't care anymore. All she wanted was to change the subject. The last thing she needed was to remind Ash of how she'd lied to him. "So..." She cleared her throat. "What's up?"

"How does Mexican sound? I know this terrific little dive about fifteen minutes from your place."

"'Terrific little dive.' Gee, how could I resist that?"

"Hey, I'll have you know dives serve some of the best food you'll ever eat."

"When are we going to eat at home? Do you realize that out of all of the meals we've eaten together, we haven't cooked even one of them?"

"What do you mean?" He sounded offended. "I cooked waffles, didn't I?"

"Eggos."

"But I cooked them."

"Toasted," she corrected. "It's not the same thing."

"Okay, if it bothers you so much, I'd be more than happy to let you make dinner tonight."

Holly thought about all of the scorched pans in her cupboards. "Actually, come to think of it, Mexican does sound good."

"That's what I thought." His voice was smug. "When should I pick you up?"

She glanced down at her bare, gooseflesh-covered legs. "Better give me an hour. I need to take a bath."

"All right, but don't get your stitches wet."

She pushed her damp bangs away from her forehead, a pointless gesture considering the downpour she'd been caught in earlier. "Too late."

"What?"

"Nothing. I'll see you in an hour."

Forty-five minutes later Ash found himself driving past Holly's house despite his attempt not to arrive early. He'd even watered the plant he'd forgotten about. Not that it would do much good, since it had been dead for a few months already.

Pride refused to let him go into the house yet, so he drove around the block. Holly lived in a fairly quiet, low-crime neighborhood. He was thankful for that. There were some parts of Denver he'd really worry if she lived in. But this was nice...well-kept yards, a few kids roller-blading, a brand new, navy blue Mercedes—oops, with a big scratch across the front bumper.

After driving around the block three times, he stopped on his next pass by her house and checked his watch. Seven-twenty. He could live with ten minutes.

When Holly opened the door, she was wearing beat-up leather tennis shoes, faded jeans with frayed hems and holes in both knees and a faded black T-shirt that had "one perce t angel, nin ty-nine percent b ch" written on it in peeling, white iron-on letters. A few letters had obviously fallen off, but Ash didn't have any difficulty filling in the blanks.

"Nice shirt."

She smiled brightly. "You like it? Paige gave it to me ages ago."

He should've guessed Paige had something to do with it.

"So what about the rest of the ensemble?" Holly turned around for his inspection. One of the belt loops was torn half way off and dangling, and there was a rip in the seat of her jeans. She was wearing flowered underwear. "Think I'm dressed okay for a dive?"

"Perfect."

The food at MexiCasa didn't disappoint. The beef enchiladas were spicy as Ash remembered, and Holly kept commenting on how shocked she was she'd actually managed to eat her entire "humongous" burrito.

He smiled as she rambled on. He'd never been bothered by her chatty streaks, and tonight he was actually thankful for them. He was perfectly content sitting back in the Naugahyde booth, keeping his mouth shut and watching her.

Somewhere along the line during the past week he'd given up fighting. His relationship with Holly may have started with lies, but the truth was he no longer cared. She swore she'd tried to confess to him a few times, and remembering back, he could see where she may have been trying to do just that. He decided to give her the benefit of the doubt.

Yes, it still hurt when he thought about her charade, but he was thinking about it less and less the more time he spent with her.

Holly brought things into his life that had previously been missing. Things like companionship and laughter and...love? Ash watched her scrape the last remnants of cheese from her plate with a taco chip. She popped it into her mouth right after once again commenting how full she was. He smiled. Maybe love wasn't that far off the mark after all.

"Are you ready to go? If I eat another chip, I'll burst, and believe me, that wouldn't be a pretty sight."

He chuckled. "Ready when you are."

He left money on the table with the bill, then followed Holly outside. The night air was a welcome change from the slightly stuffy restaurant, but the view could hardly be called romantic. From the outside, MexiCasa appeared to be nothing more than a deteriorating, squatty, stucco building situated next to the train tracks.

"It's so beautiful."

"What?" He couldn't have heard her correctly.

She pointed upward. "The sky. Look at all the stars out tonight."

Ash obliged by tilting his head back. True, there were a lot of stars. With the city lights, they usually weren't visible, but above this poorly lit, remote corner of town, the stars twinkled without artificial competition.

He was fishing keys out of his pocket when a passing car's headlights momentarily blinded him. He blinked a few times, and the spots cleared enough to catch a glimpse of a navy blue Mercedes driving away.

From the back, Ash couldn't tell if it was the same car he'd seen earlier or not. Could be coincidence; Holly's house wasn't far from the restaurant. It could be someone from her neighborhood.

"Did you make a wish?"

"A wish?"

"On the stars."

He forgot the car and focused his attention back on Holly. "Aren't you only allowed to make a wish on the first star you see, not an entire sky full?"

"Yes..." She paused, pointing west. "And I saw that one first."

He hid his grin. "What did you wish for?"

"Drive me home, and I'll tell you," she answered suggestively.

Watching the sparkle in her eyes, Ash gave her a quick kiss. "Invite me in, and I'll make sure it comes true."

CHAPTER TEN

"Paige, I tell you, we'll have to make Ash give you a ride on his motorcycle. It's so much fun."

"Fun?" Paige opened her desk drawer and pulled out a Twinkie. "Aren't you the same person who gets sick on roller coasters?"

"Roller coasters are different. I don't have a problem with speed, it's the twists and turns that always do me in."

Paige chuckled and offered her a Twinkie. "Have you had breakfast?"

"No thanks." Holly wrinkled her nose. "How can you eat that first thing in the morning?"

"What? Twinkies? They have three of the basic food groups: carbohydrates, fruit..." She indicated the strawberry filling inside. "And dairy."

"Dairy?" Holly scoffed. "Get real. There isn't any milk in those things."

"Oh no? Then what do you think this is made of?" Paige stuck her finger inside the Twinkie and scooped out a blob of filling.

Holly shuddered at the possibilities. "I don't wanna know.

I read somewhere that Twinkies can virtually last forever because there are so many preservatives in them."

"Cool."

"Paige, you're hopeless."

The phone buzzed and Paige answered it by pressing the speaker button.

"Hey, Marie. What's up?"

Marie was GDR's receptionist. "Is Holly in your office?"

"Yes, I am."

"Someone delivered a package for you."

"Thanks, Marie. I'll be right there."

She walked up to the main reception area expecting to find the new dishes she'd ordered, but the box sitting on Marie's desk was far too small to be holding twenty dog food bowls. Besides, her supplier didn't gift-wrap his shipments.

"There's a card." Marie pointed to the envelope taped to the top of the box. "Who's it from?"

She hid her grin. Marie was a terrific receptionist, but she was also the nosiest person she'd ever known—Paige excluded.

Opening the card, she read the inscription. "Thinking of you."

"It's from Ash," she said with a smile.

"Oh, how sweet." Marie fidgeted anxiously in her seat. "Open it."

Holly did as she was told, unmercifully ripping the decorative paper to shreds in the process. She had to dig through a whole mess of Styrofoam peanuts before her searching fingers touched the object hidden inside. She lifted it out of the box, ignoring the shower of peanuts that fell to the floor in the process.

"Oh, it's beautiful," Marie gasped.

Holly stared at the intricately carved mahogany box in her

hands. It was the most amazing thing she'd ever seen. Engraved on the top, a Victorian lord and lady were seated on a bench under a tree in full blossom. The sides boasted stylized hearts and fleur-de-lis, and the inside was lined with red velvet.

After turning the key on the bottom of the box, a sweet, sad, almost hypnotic melody began playing. She was mesmerized. It was as if the music reached inside her and touched her very soul.

"You be sure and give that man of yours a proper thank-you."

"I will," she promised as she floated down the hall to her office.

Seated at her desk, she dialed Ash's number while the melancholy tune played on.

"Hello?"

"I love it."

"Holly?"

"Yes. It's just breathtaking, Ash."

"That's nice. What's breathtaking?"

"My present. Can't you hear it?" She leaned down so the receiver would be closer to the music box.

Ash listened to the haunting strands of a Victorian melody. "It's pretty." Is that what she wanted to hear? "Kind of creepy, though."

"No, it's not. It's beautiful. I don't know how to thank you. No one's ever given me anything so lovely before."

Wait a minute. Something wasn't right.

"What exactly are you talking about?"

"The music box, of course. I absolutely adore it."

Music box? He suddenly felt as if he was breathing liquid. His lungs burned and his head began to swim as Jack's words echoed in his brain.

The Lyons' place was hit three days ago...they took a silver tea service, some antique music boxes...

"What did the card say?" he choked out.

"Don't you remember? It said, 'Thinking of you.'"

Ash's legs nearly buckled beneath him. How could he have missed the obvious? The hang-up phone calls, the note on her door and now the music box. Whoever sent him the locket was obviously targeting Holly now.

A wave of possessive anger coursed through his body. If anything happened to Holly, he'd kill the person responsible with his bare hands.

"Where are you? At the school?"

"Yes." She sounded confused. "Ash, what's—"

"Stay put. I'll be there as soon as I can."

He picked up his .9mm automatic and checked to make sure the clip was full. Satisfied, he stuffed the gun into the back of his jeans under the untucked T-shirt he wore and stashed an extra clip in his pocket.

"Don't go anywhere. I mean it. Not even outside to the kennels. Promise?"

"Ash, what's going on? You're freaking me out."

He looked at the golden locket sitting inside the open box on his kitchen table.

"I know how you feel."

When the phone buzzed, Holly jumped, bumping her elbow on the side of her desk. The sharp pain shot through her arm even faster than her heartbeat pounded at the base of her throat.

She winced, punched the speaker button and rubbed her sore elbow. "Hello?"

"Hi, Holly. There's a gentleman here to see you." The metallic tone of Marie's voice echoed in the quiet office.

"Tell Ash I'll be right up."

"It's not Ash."

She froze, her finger poised over the disconnect button. "It's not? Who is it?"

"His name is David Jetzel. He says he ran into your car yesterday."

Holly exhaled the breath she hadn't been aware of holding. Of course. The fender bender. She'd forgotten all about it. "Tell Mr. Jetzel I'll be with him in a minute, Marie."

She pressed the disconnect button and leaned back in her chair.

"Get a grip, Hol."

Saying the words out loud didn't trigger the hoped for response. She was still nervous. Apparently, talking to Ash had shaken her up more than she realized. She felt about as stable as a Jell-O mold in an earthquake.

She inhaled deeply, pretending not to notice the way her breath hitched as she did so, then exhaled slowly. She didn't want to keep Mr. Jetzel waiting. It wasn't very often a person was hit by someone actually willing to pay for the damages without any arguments or denials of guilt.

After checking her face in her mirrored compact—she looked a little pale, but otherwise presentable—she stashed it back in middle drawer of her desk and headed up front.

David Jetzel was standing in the lobby studying the photograph of the Great Sand Dunes National Monument that hung on the wall over the couch. He turned around to face her as she approached.

"Ever been to the Great Sand Dunes, Miss Richland?"

Holly was caught off guard by his abrupt question, but oddly enough, it relaxed her.

"No, I'm afraid I've yet to make it there."

David Jetzel shook his head in disappointment, then stopped abruptly, squinted, took off his wire-framed glasses and wiped them with a handkerchief he produced from the pocket of his navy blue blazer.

"Dust," he explained after replacing the glasses. "You really should go there at dawn."

"Excuse me?"

"The Great Sand Dunes. They are absolutely spectacular at dawn."

She felt herself smiling. From his thin, combed-over-the-bald-spot hair to his spit-polished lace-up shoes, the short, chubby man standing before her was a classic nerd in every sense of the word. She felt completely at ease with him, a welcome reaction considering the stress-filled minutes she'd spent in her office since hanging up with Ash.

"I'll have to remember that. Would you care for a cup of coffee?"

"No, thank you, Miss Richland. I don't want to take up too much of your time. If there's someplace we could talk..."

"Of course. Why don't we go into my office? Marie, could you hold my calls, please?"

She led the way to her office, motioning him inside. Consciously, she realized it was stupid to get freaked out over a phone call, yet she couldn't bring herself to close the door as she normally would have, no matter how ridiculous she felt.

Mr. Jetzel waited patiently by the chair in front of her desk. Despite her invitation, he didn't sit down until after she did.

"So Mr. Jetzel, to what do I owe the pleasure?"

"First of all, I'd like to take the opportunity to apologize again for hitting your car. It was very irresponsible of me."

"Apology accepted. These things happen."

"Not to me. I'm usually so careful—"

"Mr. Jetzel," Holly interrupted. As nice a man as he was, she was in no mood to listen to him apologize for another fifteen minutes like he had after the accident. Not when her stomach was still doing nervous flip-flops after her phone call with Ash. "What can I do for you?"

He cleared his throat. "I'm here about the damages to your car, of course. I trust you've had the opportunity to inspect it fully by now."

"Yes, I have. I was planning on calling you, but since you're here...The left taillight is broken and the back bumper is slightly dented and scratched."

He grew pale. "Oh, dear, then by all means I'll pay to replace the taillight and bumper and have the car repainted."

Holly almost laughed at his eagerness. The guy was a car crash saint. "Painting won't be necessary and the bumper isn't that bad. Just a scratch. If you'd replace the taillight, I'd be happy."

"Please, I insist on replacing the bumper as well."

She shrugged, unable to stop a giggle. "If you insist."

"I do." He pulled a business card out of his inside breast pocket and handed it to her. "Please have the repairs made and the bill sent to this address." He stood. "I won't take any more of your time."

She rose and shook the hand he extended.

"Again, I truly am sorry for any inconvenience I've caused." When she started to walk around the desk, he added, "I can show myself out. Goodbye, Miss Richland."

"Goodbye."

Holly stared at the card in her hand. The words "Stellar Incorporated" winked back at her in silver embossed letters. Now she understood why Mr. Jetzel was so meticulous. He was vice-president of a company that only hired the best certified public accountants in the business. Denver's most prestigious corporations turned to Stellar for their expertise.

The phone buzzed, and she absently hit the button. "Hey, Marie."

"I asked him to wait, but he walked right past me."

"Who walked past you?"

"Me."

She turned around to find Ash standing in her office doorway. Her heart skipped a beat, like it did every time she saw him. "It's okay, Marie," she reassured the receptionist.

"Where's the music box?"

"Hello to you too." She planted her hands firmly on her hips and glared at him. "Just what do you mean by scaring the hell out of me on the phone?"

"Sorry. You all right?"

"Except for the fact I've been looking over my shoulder for the past half hour every time I hear a noise, yes, I'm fine."

He visibly relaxed at her words, then crossed the room, took a Kleenex out of the box on her desk, used it to pick up the music box and began inspecting it.

"Did anyone else touch this?"

"No. What's going on?"

He was starting to scare her again. His actions reminded her of the other night when FedEx had delivered the locket.

"I'm not sure yet."

No way. He was not going to give her the brush off again.

"Well, you'd better figure something out pretty quick, because I deserve an answer, and we're not going anywhere until I get one."

He looked at her a hard minute, then sighed heavily. "This music box is stolen."

"What?"

"It was stolen on Friday from a private residence."

Holly couldn't believe what she was hearing. "How do you know that?"

"I just do."

"Uh-uh." She shook her head. "That's not going to cut it this time. What aren't you telling me?"

After a moment of apparently trying to stare her down—she forced herself not to look away—he walked over to close and lock the door. When he didn't turn around immediately, she swallowed the fear rising in her throat.

"Ash?" Her voice sounded hollow and fragile, even to her own ears.

"I think someone's after you."

The bluntness of his words made her wish he hadn't decided to talk. A chill crawled over her skin, and she laughed nervously.

"Excuse me?"

"I'm not sure who, but I think they're trying to get to me through you."

"Wait a minute. Wait a minute." She avoided his attempt to hold her and started pacing around her office. "You're not making sense."

"None of your friends left that note on your door."

"You don't know that," she countered. "I haven't asked any of them, yet."

"Paige didn't call you and hang up."

"Just because she won't confess doesn't mean she didn't do it."

"I didn't send you this music box." Ash held it up and shook it for effect. "So who did?"

Holly stopped pacing and stared at the Victorian music box in his outstretched hand. Her nose tickled as tears welled in her eyes.

"Who?" he shouted.

She flinched and shouted back, "I don't know!"

Ash put down the music box and folded his arms around her. "That's what I was afraid of."

She burrowed against him like a lost child who'd just been found, wrapping her arms around his waist. When she touched the gun stuffed into the waistband of his jeans, she pulled back and looked up at him in shock. No matter how badly she wanted to pretend Ash hadn't said any of the things she'd just heard, the presence of his gun forced her to admit he had.

"This has something to do with that locket, doesn't it?"

He nodded slowly.

"What's so special about that locket? Who does it belong to?"

He kissed her forehead, then held her more firmly against his chest, as if trying to shield her from whatever he was about to say.

"It belonged to a hostage who was murdered."

The girl pictured in the locket. From the way Ash spoke the words and the tremor that ran through his body, Holly knew he blamed himself for the girl's death. That must be why he quit the force.

"And the guy who shot her is after me now?"

She felt his head shake of denial rather than saw it. "He's dead."

"Then who—?"

"I don't know. We thought he was a run of the mill embezzler who went off the deep end, but apparently he wasn't working alone." Ash tightened his arms around her. "Someone sent me that locket."

She shivered. That same someone was sending her

presents and leaving notes on her door. Her stomach twisted violently.

"He knows where I live."

"That's why you need to stay at my apartment until I figure this out."

She nodded her agreement.

"Good girl. Let's get out of here. Can you take the rest of the day off?"

"Yes, but..."

"But what?"

"What about Riley? He's on a deadline."

"Riley will do fine without you."

Not likely. Carmen sure as heck wasn't going to work with him.

"But Ash..."

Pushing her an arm's length away, Ash stared down in disapproval. "Holly, you come first."

The determination and conviction in his eyes melted any protests before they passed her lips. "Okay," she agreed. "We'll play by your rules."

They were walking across the gravel driveway to Ash's motorcycle when Holly stopped abruptly.

"What is it?"

"My car. Should I leave it here?"

Ash followed her gaze to the white Ford Taurus parked a few feet away.

"What happened to the bumper?"

"Oh, some guy ran into me at a stoplight yesterday."

"What?" He shot her an accusing look. "You were in an accident? Why didn't you tell me?"

"It wasn't a big deal. Besides, the guy's paying to get it fixed."

Ash focused his attention back on the bumper, and his pulse quickened. He walked over, knelt down and examined the scratches.

"What kind of car?"

"What kind? A brand new Mercedes that puts my old car to shame."

A streak of color stood out boldly on the white bumper, confirming his suspicions. He traced it with his fingers. "Navy blue."

"Yes."

He shut his eyes tightly. What was wrong with him? He should've listened to his instincts when he saw that car drive by MexiCasa last night.

"Do you know the guy's name?"

"Sure, he dropped by today and left me his business card."

Ash stood abruptly and spun around to face her. "He was *here*?"

She raised an eyebrow. "I just said that."

"When?"

"Right before you."

Dammit! Why didn't he drive faster?

"Where's his card?"

"I know what you're thinking, but he was–"

"Holly."

Obviously deciding to humor him, she reached into her purse and pulled out a gray linen business card. He snatched it from her grasp and read the inscription. The fact that Stellar Incorporated represented accountants and Gina Lyons' murderer was an accountant was too much of a coincidence for him.

"What's the matter? You don't really believe Mr. Jetzel has anything to do with this, do you?"

"I'm not counting him out." He stuffed the business card into the back pocket of his jeans, then took Holly by the hand and led her toward his bike. "Leave your car here. I want you with me."

∽

Holly adjusted her grip and held on to Ash more tightly. He was driving fast—faster than he usually drove—and it scared her. Not because she doubted his ability to handle the monster Harley, but because she could feel the tension in his body.

Even when they stopped by her house to make sure Bryton had enough food and water, he didn't relax. He paced back and forth from the front window to the back porch the entire five minutes they were there, constantly urging her to speed things up. She was barely able to grab a change of clothes before he dragged her out of the house, and they were moving again.

They reached his apartment shortly after noon. He locked the door behind them, closed all the blinds and was on the phone with Jack before Holly could utter a word. She watched in semi-amazement as Ash hounded him until he gave in and promised to run Mr. Jetzel and Stellar Incorporated through the police computer.

"Jack's going to call me back. It shouldn't take long."

Holly deliberately let her gaze fall to the phone he still held in his hand. He was gripping it so tightly, his knuckles showed white. She pried it from his fingers and set it on the coffee table.

"You can pick it back up when it rings," she informed him. "Now come and sit down." She tried to lead him to the couch, but he stood immobile. Sighing, she eyed him crookedly as he frowned. "Ash, try to relax."

"I can't relax."

"Well, you'd better or you're going to bust a vein in your forehead."

His frown deepened, but otherwise he didn't move.

"You can't blame yourself," she said, abandoning her futile attempt to make him budge. She walked to the couch. "I'm sure you weren't responsible for her death."

Like a statue come to life, his hand shot out to grab her upper arm, preventing her from sitting. "What did you say?"

Holly looked at his fingers digging into her flesh, and he instantly released her. "The hostage," she said carefully. "Her death wasn't your fault."

Pain crossed his features as noticeably as a shadow. "You weren't there."

"I didn't have to be. I know you. And you wouldn't stand by and let someone die."

She wasn't prepared for Ash's laughter. The hollow, life-less sound was unnerving.

"You don't know me very well then, because that's exactly what I did."

She shook her head. "I don't believe it."

"Believe it."

His eyes reminded her of a National Geographic special where a timber wolf was caught in a trap. The look of help-less, unmasked terror she'd seen in the animal was mirrored in Ash's wild gaze.

"I could've shot him, but instead, I put my gun down and let him kill her."

"You're wrong."

"Dammit, Holly! I know what happened."

She flinched at the force of his words, but didn't back down. "No."

Ash furrowed his brows and stared in amazement at the woman standing stubbornly before him. He wasn't sure if he wanted to kiss her for having faith in him or strangle her for being so damned stupid. She didn't know what happened, because she wasn't there. He was. And he remembered every horrible, nauseating detail as if it was yesterday.

When Holly placed a hand on his cheek, he stiffened, yet couldn't bring himself to pull away. Her touch felt too good to abandon.

"I don't care what you say. Argue all night if you want to, but you didn't make that guy pull the trigger. He did that. Not you. Him."

Ash shut his eyes tightly. "I should've stopped him. God, she was just a kid. I—" His voice cracked, and he stopped abruptly, mortified by his lack of control.

When Holly's lips touched his, he opened his eyes to find her watching him. Her warm gaze was as soft as her mouth, and tears he hadn't noticed before clung to her lashes, making them appear spiky.

With a groan, he pulled her against his chest and deepened the kiss. His guilt and fear made the embrace a cry of pain and when he finally pulled back, tears were flowing freely down her cheeks.

"I'm sorry," she said in a broken whisper.

"No, baby, I'm sorry. Did I hurt—"

She halted his words with a kiss, cupping his face with both her hands, urging his lips apart with her tongue. He opened his mouth to her, greedily taking everything she offered, marveling at the way the ache in his chest seemed to lessen with each tender stoke of her tongue.

"I'm sorry you had to go through that," she mouthed

against his lips. "I'm sorry that girl died." She kissed him again, desperately, fiercely. "But it wasn't your fault. You have to let it go before it destroys you."

He wanted to believe her. He wanted to forget with every fiber of his being, but the memories wouldn't let go. They held on with iron jaws, shredding his emotions, tearing away strips of his soul.

Holly wrapped her arms around his neck and hugged him tightly. He buried his face in the hollow between her neck and shoulder and held on for dear life.

"It's okay," she whispered.

But it wasn't okay. Gina Lyons was dead and there was nothing he could do to bring her back. He couldn't change the past, but he could prevent it from repeating itself with Holly.

"Promise me something?"

"What?"

"Promise you'll stay here."

"I'll stay as long as you want me to."

He kissed her neck, then pulled back to look into her eyes, trying to convey how important his next request was. "Promise you won't go anywhere without me until I get this figured out?"

"Ash, it's probably nothing."

"Then it won't take long," he countered. "Promise."

"Well..."

"Please."

"If it means that much to you."

"It does."

"All right. I promise."

He exhaled his relief in a rush of air. "Thank you."

Ash intended his kiss to be one of gratitude, but now that some of the tension had left his body, there was room for other feelings. Holly's lips parted under his, and desire leapt to the forefront. He tilted his head and deepened the kiss, thrusting his tongue into the sweet warmth of her mouth as he grasped her butt and pulled her against him. It wasn't close enough, so he gripped her leg behind the knee, lifted it nearly to his waist and rocked his hips into hers. Holly moaned, and the sound spurred him. He ran his hand along the silk of her bare skin, beneath the flowery material of her mid-thigh skirt and worked his fingers under the lace of her panties. She broke their kiss with a gasp.

God he loved it when she caught her breath. It was a tell-tale sign she was starting to lose control, and he wanted her out of control...begging him not to stop.

Ash reclaimed her mouth and continued to stoke her, sliding a finger into her warmth. She gasped again, then shut her eyes and caught her bottom lip with her teeth. After a beat, her eyes fluttered open to meet his with a look so sultry, he literally had to remind himself to breathe.

God, she was so damn sexy.

Exhaling on a groan, he lifted and carried her to the wall a few steps away where he set her down, back against the wall. Inching her panties down her legs, he knelt on the carpet and grasped her calf. She lifted her foot at his urging, and the lace slipped down her toes to the floor. She started to put her foot down, but instead of letting go, he tossed her leg over his shoulder, lifted her skirt and kissed her intimately.

Holly slammed against the wall, splaying her fingers and reaching her hands outward along the textured sheetrock in search of support as his lips and tongue devoured her. He could feel her jerk ever so slightly whenever he'd change from circling his tongue to flicking up and down, and her breath would hitch. The more he worked her, the more frequent the jerks became. He knew she was getting close. So when she twined her fingers in his hair and tugged, he reluctantly looked up for an explanation.

"Not without you," she told him, sliding her leg off his shoulder. It hit the floor with all the stability of a slinky, and she swayed into him once he stood.

When she began undoing the button fly of his jeans, Ash lifted his shirt out of the way, not wanting anything to interfere with her progress. She laughed at his eagerness, but he didn't care. He was eager, and with her hands on his crotch, there was no way she couldn't tell.

The denim barely hit the floor before she was backing him toward the couch. Ash stepped out of his jeans and jockey shorts just before his heels hit the sofa. She pushed him down onto it and straddled him. Her flowy skirt was pillowed around her, but he knew she couldn't be positioned more than a mere inch or two above his erection. Even so, he forced himself not to move, because no matter how badly he needed to be inside her, he wanted to let her remain in control.

Holly leaned forward and placed her hands on his chest to steady herself. When she lowered her hips a fraction, her heat brushing against him, he sucked in a sharp breath with a hiss, an almost pained expression on his face.

A smile tugged at the corner of her lips; the wicked glint in her eyes letting him know she was enjoying making him wait.

When her hair spilled onto his shoulder, leaving the soft scent of coconut shampoo in its wake, he clenched his teeth, using every last shred of restraint to keep from thrusting into her.

Without a word, she covered his mouth with hers and pushed downward. Ash groaned and surged upward to meet her, grasping her hips to hold her in place.

Holly rocked against him, sheathing him completely in her warmth. He responded by lifting her, then pulling her down hard. After that, he was lost in a whirlwind of movement and sensation. Nothing mattered but going deeper, moving faster.

They were both sweaty and clinging to one another when the release finally came. Holly collapsed onto him as the last of her inner tremors subsided.

He brushed a damp strand of her hair away to kiss her forehead, the blood still humming in his veins. There was so much he felt, so much he wanted to say...

"Wow." Not exactly what he'd intended to say, but it did make her giggle.

"Better than Disneyland?"

He laughed. "Better than Disneyland." Without warning, he rolled her underneath him and ground his hips against hers. "And no wait."

CHAPTER ELEVEN

The phone rang, shattering the relaxed state Ash had been lulled into by their lovemaking. Holly was asleep on his chest, so he slowly leaned forward to pick it up, then eased back against the couch cushions, trying not to wake her. "Hello?"

"Malone? I've got that info you wanted."

He instantly tensed at the sound of Jack's voice. "And?"

"Jetzel's cleaner than the soles of a hooker's shoes. Not even a traffic violation."

"Damn. What about Stellar?"

"Same tune, different lyrics. Only scratch on their perfect record is that Grainger Technology hired Donald Craig through them."

"Donald Craig." His blood ran cold...Bad Suit. "Don't tell me we overlooked Stellar."

"We didn't. I checked them out myself while you were dealing with the Lyons. Don't you remember?"

The only thing Ash remembered clearly about the week between the shooting and the funeral was the image of Gina Lyons lying in a pool of her own blood.

"Refresh my memory."

"Nothing to tell. Stellar was clean. Their CEO even paid for the girl's funeral."

Ash massaged the throbbing at the bridge of his nose. "It's too neat. We're missing something. I can feel it."

"Maybe you're looking for something that isn't there," Jack began hesitantly. "Maybe Jetzel really did accidently hit the gas instead of the brakes. There's nothing to suggest he's after Holly."

"It doesn't feel right. I can't..." Ash shook his head decisively. "Dammit, it doesn't feel right."

"I'll keep my eyes and ears open."

"I need you to do one more thing."

There was a pause, followed by a hesitant, "What?"

"Check the music box for prints and run them through N.C.I.C."

Jack's voice echoed of resigned compliance. "Fine. Drop it by the station."

"Will do. Thanks, man, I owe you." He was about to hang up, when Jack's words stopped him.

"Malone? Watch your step. You're not toting a badge anymore."

Ash paused briefly before hanging up. He tossed the phone onto the coffee table and leaned his head back against the couch cushion to stare at the ceiling.

"What's wrong?"

Looking down, he found Holly watching him. "How long have you been awake?"

"Not long. What did Jack say?"

He shrugged and stared back at the ceiling.

"Is Mr. Jetzel wanted by the police?"

"No." Just by one ex-cop, he added silently. There were too many questions needing answers.

131

Holly's breath tickled his neck. "Good. He's so nice. It's hard to believe he'd want to hurt anyone."

Yeah, nice. Too nice for his liking. The puzzle piece didn't fit, no matter how badly Jack and Holly wanted it to.

"I've got to go out for a while. Will you stay here until I get back?"

"Where're you going?"

He avoided her probing gaze. "I haven't been to the grocery store in over a week."

"We could order a pizza."

Maneuvering Holly so she was sitting upright on the couch and no longer reclining across his chest, Ash stood, retrieved his jeans and pulled them on. "I don't want the pizza joint to get too dependent on me."

"Then I'll come with you." She pushed herself off the couch to stand. Her floral-print skirt swirled down into place around her thighs.

"You're not wearing any underwear," he reminded her, kissing her softly. "Besides, you're safer here as long as you promise not to answer the door." He stepped into his boots one at a time, then turned and walked through the kitchen.

"Stellar Incorporated is on the other end of town. Will you be back before five?"

Ash stopped in his tracks. Sometimes she was too damn smart for her own good. Turning, he looked Holly straight in the eye. "I'll try. Promise not to answer the door?"

"Will you buy me some Doritos at the grocery store?"

He felt his lips twitch. "Deal."

"I don't care if he's with the President of the United States. I'm not leaving until I see him."

Ash's voice echoed throughout the cavernous lobby of the Stellar Incorporated offices, prompting the receptionist to screw her mouth into a tight-lipped frown and glare at him. She wasn't easy on the eyes to begin with, but with her face pinched in disapproval, she could probably scare a gargoyle into submission.

"Mr. Malone, I'm sorry, but I have strict orders that Mr. Jetzel is not to be disturbed."

"What seems to be the problem here, Bernice?"

"Oh, Mr. Desmond. I didn't know you were here, sir."

Ash watched in amazement as the grotesque, snarling creature behind the desk practically melted into a giggling, homely schoolgirl before his eyes. She'd called the man 'sir.' Desmond must be the big cheese at Stellar, and it was quite obvious Bernice here had a huge crush on him.

"This gentleman is insisting upon seeing Mr. Jetzel, even though I've repeatedly assured him he's unavailable."

"Perhaps I may be of assistance, Mr..."

"Malone," Ash supplied, sizing the guy up through narrowed eyes. He was tall—he had at least two inches on him—and slender. One of those pretty boy, model types who never had a hair out of place, always dressed impeccably and probably matched his socks to his shorts. He disliked him on sight.

"Malone," the man echoed, stepping around the receptionist's desk to extend his well-manicured hand. "I'm Frank Desmond, Chief Executive Officer of Stellar Incorporated."

Ash shook his hand, appalled by the CEO's weak grip and soft skin. He reminded him of a vampire: cold, calculating, and bloodless. No wonder the gargoyle was so taken with him.

"Maybe you can help me, Frank. Do you mind if I call you Frank?"

Dracula shook his head politely, but the gargoyle glowered at Ash from behind her desk. He avoided her beady-eyed stare.

"Is there someplace private we can talk, Frank?"

"Certainly. Why don't we step into the board room?"

"Lead the way."

The board room was long and narrow, just wide enough to fit a massive, black lacquer table with twenty chairs surrounding it. Ash glanced at the shiny surface and saw Frank Desmond's image reflected next to his own. *Huh. Didn't think vampires had reflections.*

"That's my mother, Stella Desmond. God rest her soul."

Ash looked up to find Desmond smiling sadly at the portrait hanging on the far wall behind the chair at the head of the table.

"I started the company shortly after her death. It's named in her honor."

When Desmond pulled out a chair and motioned for him to do the same, Ash walked around to the other side of the table and took the seat opposite.

"So Mr. Malone, what interest does Stellar hold for the police department?"

Ash lounged back in his seat. Desmond assumed he was working with the police. Good. Now he wouldn't have to produce the badge he no longer possessed. "Can't sneak much past you, Frankie."

"This doesn't have anything to do with that unfortunate shooting last month does it? Because, as I told the officers then, we screen our people as best we can, but Stellar obviously can't be held accountable for the personal actions of the accountants we employ."

Ash narrowed his eyes. The guy was a master of smooth talking. Every even-tempered word, every sedate inflection was probably chosen to soothe the listener. Ash found it had the exact opposite effect on him.

"Of course not," he said gruffly. "But that's not why I'm here."

"It's not?" Desmond seemed disappointed he wasn't going to be given the opportunity to defend his company against potentially slanderous remarks. "Then why did you come?"

"Your vice-president was involved in an accident with a friend of mine. I wanted to ask him a few questions, but that–" He checked himself. "Your receptionist refused to let me see him."

"David Jetzel is a very busy man, but I assure you, Stellar will pay for any damages to your friend's car. She wasn't hurt, I trust?"

"She?"

"Pardon me?"

"You said *she* wasn't hurt. How did you know my friend is a woman?"

Desmond's smile revealed perfectly even, impossibly white teeth. Probably veneers.

"You, Mr. Malone, strike me as a lady's man. I'm sure you have quite a few women friends, if you'll forgive the assumption."

Ash stared at him until Desmond broke eye contact. "No. She wasn't hurt. Just the car."

"I'm relieved to hear it, and as I said, we'll pay for the damages. Now…" He pushed himself up from the table. "If there isn't anything else you'd like to discuss, I have some business to attend to."

Ignoring the blatant dismissal, Ash didn't make any attempt to stand. "Actually, Frankie…" He leaned back in his chair. "I do have more questions."

The CEO reluctantly sat back down.

"Someone's been leaving my friend disturbing notes. You don't suppose your Mr. Jetzel would know anything about that, do you?"

"Definitely not."

"See, the funny thing is she didn't start receiving them until after your vice-president rammed into her car. A little too coincidental, don't you think?"

"Are you implying that David is sending your friend threatening notes? Because, I assure you, that's ridiculous."

"Is it?"

"Completely. David Jetzel is a fine, upstanding citizen. He's been with me for years. He would never harass anyone."

"Maybe you're right, Frankie, and maybe you're not. I want the notes to stop. I won't put up with anyone bothering my friend." Ash rose to his feet, never taking his eyes off the man across from him. He was certain Desmond was capable of lying to cover for Stellar's vice-president. He just wasn't sure yet if the guy was actually guilty. "Tell Mr. Jetzel I'm sorry I missed him."

He was reaching for the door-knob when Desmond spoke. "It's a shame, it really is."

"The car?"

Desmond swiveled his chair around so he was facing him and shook his head. "The girl who was shot. How terrible for her young life to end so tragically."

Ash clenched his teeth, gave one brief nod and left.

"Ash, you haven't touched your spaghetti. I know I'm not much of a cook," Holly admitted, "but I can boil water. I can also tell when something's bothering you."

"I'm fine," he assured her. "The spaghetti's great."

She stared pointedly at his fork. It was still lying, untouched, on top of his folded paper napkin.

"Great," she echoed. "Are you ever going to tell me what happened at Stellar?"

He pushed his chair back from the table and walked to the refrigerator to get another beer. The cap twisted off with a pop, and he drank a long swallow.

"Nothing happened." He shrugged and tossed the bottle cap into the paper bag on the floor that was doubling as a garbage can. "Jetzel wasn't there."

Holly was relieved. David Jetzel wouldn't hurt a fly. She was certain of it. "Maybe that's for the best. You–"

"I did talk to the CEO."

She was almost afraid to ask. "What did you say?"

He sat back down at the table. "I told him Jetzel needed to stop sending you notes."

Her fork dropped to her plate with a clank. "Ash! You can't just run around accusing people without–"

"Probable cause? I've got it. Do you know sweet Mr. Jetzel has been following you around town in that navy blue Mercedes of his?"

"What? Don't be silly."

"It's true. I saw it by your house the other night and again at the restaurant."

"Do you know how many navy blue Mercedes there are in Denver?"

"Plenty." He pointed at her. "But not with a scratched front bumper."

"So what? Do you know how many bad drivers there are in Denver?" Didn't he know how ridiculous he sounded? "It was just a fender bender. Look..." She pushed her hair behind her ears. "I'm not denying the existence of those notes. All

I'm saying is it's very possible someone other than Mr. Jetzel wrote them."

Ash groaned, rubbing his forehead. "You're right. It's just so damned frustrating not knowing who it is. I feel so—" He stopped abruptly. After a moment, he reached across the table to take her hand in his. "I don't want anything to happen to you."

"Nothing will." She squeezed his fingers. "You're here to protect me," she added, even though she wasn't totally convinced she was actually in danger. Oh, she had no doubt Ash believed she was and that was unnerving in itself. After all, he was a trained SWAT officer, and from everything she knew about that division of the police force, they didn't scare easily.

Still, all she'd received was a couple of, in truth, non-threatening notes and an apparently stolen music box. She'd be the first to admit she wasn't drop dead gorgeous, but maybe she just had a secret admirer with sticky fingers. Nothing indicated anyone wanted to hurt her, like he seemed to think.

"Don't forget what you promised."

"Not to go anywhere without you," she replied automatically. She'd repeated that so many times, it could be a mantra. After a few moments of silence, she ran her tongue suggestively across her upper lip and slowly raised her gaze to his. "I suppose, then, I should tell you I'm planning on going into the bedroom."

A smile played at the corners of his mouth. "You are?"

"Uh-huh. And once I get there, I'm afraid I'm going to have to take off all of my clothes..." She paused for effect. "And then climb into bed. But I'm sure you didn't mean you'd have to go there with me too, did you?"

He shook his head and clucked his tongue. "Afraid so."

"Oh." Holly tried to look depressed, but had a feeling she failed miserably. "Then I guess you'd better follow me on back−" She undid a button on her shirt. "−because I'm really−" Another button. "−really−" One more. "−sleepy." She pushed her shirt off her shoulders and let it slide down her arms to the floor. Her nipples hardened when Ash's gaze raked over her breasts.

"Then by all means, you'd better get to bed."

She slipped off one bra strap. "Tuck me in?"

Ash reached across to push her other bra strap off her shoulder. "What do you think?"

In that heavenly plateau between sleep and waking, Holly smelled...spaghetti?

She opened her eyes and squinted at the clock on the nightstand. Nine-forty-five. Rolling over, she found Ash propped up in bed, eating cold spaghetti from a plate on his lap. It was a chipped Pfaltzgraff dinner plate−not a fig leaf−but it did conceal all the vital parts.

She had to smile. "What are you doing?"

"I never got to finish dinner. I was hungry."

"You never started dinner," she corrected.

He took another bite of spaghetti, licking the sauce from his lips.

"Can I have a bite?"

He shook his head. "Get your own plate."

"Mine's in the kitchen," she whined. "It's cold in the kitchen."

"I know. I was in there when I got my plate. Don't worry, you'll survive it."

The thought of leaving the toasty warmth of the covers was too distasteful, so she decided to try a different tack.

"Please? I'll make it worth your while."

He shot her a sideways glance. "What would you do for a bite?"

"This." Stretching upward, she swirled her tongue around his ear until she felt him shiver.

"Okay. One bite."

He fed her a forkful of spaghetti. It tasted so good, she asked for another.

"No."

"Don't be so selfish."

"I'm not. I'll give you another bite, but I get one first."

She let out an exaggerated sigh as he was about to put the food in his mouth, hoping he'd take pity on her. Apparently it worked, because he stopped abruptly and pointed the fork toward her. She leaned forward and opened her mouth, but wasn't prepared when he deliberately tipped the fork downward. Spaghetti spilled onto her bare breasts.

His smug smile reminded her of a pirate's. "I'll get that," he announced gallantly before bending his head.

Ash lifted a strand of spaghetti off her skin with his tongue, then sucked it into his mouth. The noodle slithered across her breast, leaving a trail of sauce in its wake. He then proceeded to lick off the sauce trail, before moving to the next piece of spaghetti.

By the time he'd eaten the entire forkful and licked the sauce clean, Holly was incredibly warm.

"You make a great plate, my dear, but fair is fair. Would you like another bite? It is your turn."

She shook her head, feeling flushed and incredibly aroused. "You're bigger than me. I think you'd better have another one first."

"Maybe you're right." He flashed a devilish grin. "I am still hungry." There was no mistaking the double entendre in his tone.

By the time they'd finished the plate of spaghetti, every inch of Holly's skin was tingling, sauce was everywhere, and she was so turned on, she could barely stand it. She needed him inside her, and she needed him now.

"Ash." His name came out as a plea.

"What baby?" He was propped up on his elbow, watching her. "What do you want?"

"You know what I want." She was wound so tightly, she was actually trembling with need. Her hips started undulating of their own accord, trying to relieve the ache between her thighs. She tried to pull him to her, but he resisted.

"Show me what you want." His voice was low, intoxicating.

Holly could see the beads of perspiration on his brow, hear the waver in his voice, feel the intensity of his stare. He needed her as badly as she needed him, she was sure of it. She reached over and slid her hand down his abdomen, moving ever lower. When he stopped her, grasping and holding her wrist, she shot him a questioning look.

His eyes darkened as his gaze locked with hers. After a moment, he lifted her hand to his lips, sucked her fingers into his mouth and circled them with his tongue. Her breath caught in her throat as he slowly pulled them out and guided her hand to the triangle between her legs.

"Show me," he commanded, before his eyes played down the length of her to watch.

Oh god.

She felt herself blush and swallowed hard.

"I said, show me."

Holly drew her lips into her mouth and bit down with her

teeth. Summoning her resolve, she released them on a slow exhale, closed her eyes and touched herself.

Ash groaned.

The guttural sound sent a jolt of fire through her veins, melting away her self-consciousness. She began stroking... slowly...up and down...on her most sensitive spot.

His whispered, "Sweet Jesus" drew a soft moan from her lips. It was so incredibly erotic with him watching her. She felt naughty and brazen and so damn hot. Ash began fondling her breast, rolling her pebbled nipple between his fingers. She moaned again and quickened her pace. The knot in her core coiled tighter, forcing her breath out in short huffs. She was so damn close.

When she felt his hand leave her breast and caress her inner thigh, she shattered instantly, arching her back and crying out, lost in the tempest that shook her.

Once her breathing slowed, her eyes fluttered open to find Ash shaking his head in wonder. His eyes were a deep, stormy blue.

"You're incredible." He kissed her softly before positioning himself between her legs and entering her.

Their lovemaking was slow and tender. Ash took his time, as if savoring the feel of her beneath him, around him. He sprinkled kisses on her lips, her cheek, her neck, and entwined his fingers with hers. He made her feel adored and treasured, like no man ever had before.

Relishing the calm bliss that follows exquisite love making, Holly lightly ran her fingers along his back, making lazy patterns on his skin.

"Mmm, that feels good." He kissed her neck, then propped up on his elbows. When he tried to roll off to her side, however, she protested.

"Wait." She loved having his weight pressing down on her, loved having him so close. "Don't move."

"I've got to be squashing you."

"You're not," she assured him. "You're fine. Better than fine. You're perfect."

Ash laughed. "You're crazy."

"Crazy about you."

Whoa, did she just say that out loud? What was wrong with her?

"I mean...I like you," she backpedaled. "We have fun together. Don't we? Not that I'm implying I don't think you're enjoying yourself as much as I am. I do...I mean, I hope you are...I mean—"

Ash silenced her babbling with a kiss. "Holly, relax. I know what you mean." He kissed her again, slowly, thoroughly. "Quite a lot, actually. To me, that is."

She smiled. "Me too." Wait. That didn't sound right. "I mean—"

"I know," he whispered against her lips before drugging her with another kiss.

When his mouth finally lifted from hers, she sighed happily. "Okay, now move." She punctuated the order with a small push.

"Why? I thought you were crazy about me."

She rolled her eyes in response to his smug expression. "Because," she began, lightly bussing the tip of his nose, "I know I saw you unpack a banana cream pie with the rest of the groceries...and it's time for dessert."

CHAPTER TWELVE

"Watch it, will you?" Ash rubbed the back of his head. "That thing smarts."

"One run-through, that's all I'm asking. Riley's on a deadline."

"I know he's on a deadline. All you've talked about for the last half hour is Riley's deadline, but I still don't think it's a good idea." He ducked, missing Holly's next swipe of the magazine by a mere inch or two judging from the wind that ruffled his hair.

"Four days. I've been cooped up in this apartment for four days."

"That's not completely true. We went to the doctor's office to get your stitches removed yesterday...Ow!"

That's it. He was cancelling his subscription to Sports Illustrated.

"This is so stupid. No one's after me."

"That's what they want you to think." Immediately after speaking the words, Ash leapt from the couch before Holly could deck him again.

"No, that's the truth." She dropped the magazine onto the

couch and began counting off fingers. "There haven't been any more notes, no more packages, no one's called and no one's come to the door..." She uncurled her pinky. "And the only fingerprints Jack found on the music box were mine." She held her open hand up for his inspection. "No more reasons to stay locked inside."

"You're overlooking the obvious. Who in their right mind wipes a gift clean of fingerprints before putting it into a box and mailing it?"

"That's beside the point."

"No one. The answer is no one." He paused a moment, allowing his words to sink in. "Not unless they have something to hide."

Holly spun around with a frustrated groan. She stood with her back to him for a long while. Even so, he was able to recognize the exact moment when the fight left her. Shoulders slumped, she sat on the couch back. Ash knelt on the cushions behind her and wrapped his arms around her waist.

"I know you're going stir-crazy—"

"That's the understatement of the year."

"But I'd rather deal with that than how I'd feel if something happened to you."

She sighed heavily. "Nothing is going to happen to me. How much longer is it going to take for you to believe that?"

He didn't know how to answer that one. In all honesty, he was beginning to wonder if he was overreacting. Holly was right. Absolutely nothing suspicious had happened since the delivery of the music box. He really couldn't blame her for being antsy, but he also couldn't shake the feeling he'd learned to trust during his years on the force, the one that sat in his gut like a lead weight, refusing to believe everything was on the up and up.

"Tell you what. Let me talk to Jack. If he hasn't heard anything, maybe I'll reconsider." *Maybe.*

She relaxed against him. "You mean it?"

"Yeah. So, you think you can hang in there one more day?"

"One more day?" She stiffened and pulled away from him. "What do you mean one more day? Why can't you call him now?"

"He's off today. It's his kid's birthday."

She glared at him, so he offered a compromise. "I suppose I could ask him a few questions after I give Dylan his present."

"Wait a minute. You're going to the party?"

"I have to. I'm the godfather."

"Can I come?"

Ash shook his head.

"Why not?"

"A house full of six-year-olds is not the best place to keep an eye on you. Besides, they think you're blind, remember?"

"Jack knows I'm not blind."

"But Elaine doesn't, and I'd rather not tell her in the middle of her son's party."

"But—"

"Holly."

"So I'll pretend to be blind. I've done it before."

That comment stung a little. "All I'm asking for is an hour."

She furrowed her brows.

"What's one hour compared to four days?" He tried to sound nonchalant, but he wasn't going to back down no matter what she said.

"Fine. I'll give you your hour, but you'd better not take any longer."

"I won't. Stay here. Promise?"

She stared at the chipped polish on her toenails. "I know the drill."

Ash got off the couch, walked around it and kissed her. "Hang in there, okay?"

"Okay, I will...For one hour."

Ninety minutes later, Ash still hadn't returned. He was probably eating cake and ice cream, figuring she'd cooled down and forgotten their entire conversation by now.

Holly glanced at her watch again. This was ridiculous. Here she'd spent the last hour and a half peeling the polish off her toenails while Riley rotted away in his kennel. She'd called Paige earlier to see how he was doing and found out Carmen hadn't worked with him once, not once since she'd been stuck in this apartment.

"Why are you surprised?" she asked herself out loud.

Riley only had three days left before Carmen cut him from the program. She never did believe Riley had what it took to become a guide dog, but she was wrong.

So, prove it, a voice inside her head challenged. You gave Ash more than his allotted hour, and you never did actually promise to stay in the apartment longer than that.

"That's right." A smile touched her lips. "I didn't, did I?"

Since her car was at the school, Holly called an Uber before putting on her socks and tennis shoes. She scribbled out a note for Ash and stuck it to the refrigerator with a Pizza Hut magnet, then walked outside to wait for the ride.

Gone for a walk. Hope you enjoyed the cake. – Holly

Ash crumpled up the piece of paper and hurled it across the living room.

"Dammit, dammit, dammit!"

He checked his watch and swore again. Fifty minutes. He was only fifty minutes late. Why on earth did he have to fall for a woman who was so damned stubborn?

The fact Jack hadn't turned up anything new on Jetzel was beside the point. Holly didn't know that, yet she'd still refused to stay put and wait like she'd promised. He should've realized she'd take his estimated arrival time of one hour literally. She probably stepped out the door at exactly minute sixty-one.

"Dammit!"

He snatched his keys from the tabletop where he'd tossed them and exited his apartment, slamming the door forcefully enough the bang echoed in the concrete stairwell.

CHAPTER THIRTEEN

Riley stopped abruptly and Holly opened her eyes. Before them lay a huge puddle which spanned the entire width of the sidewalk. With a shriek of delight, she knelt down and hugged the dog.

"What a good boy, Riley. You're such a good boy."

Progress. That's what this puddle represented. Riley was making progress. All of a sudden, she didn't feel quite so guilty about leaving the apartment without Ash.

"Come on, boy. Let's keep going."

She stood after administering one more scratch behind the dog's ear. Before she could give the "forward" command, however, someone tapped her on the back.

"Pardon me, but do you know the way to forgiveness?"

Holly wrinkled her brows. "What?"

She started to turn around, but the man poked her in the back again. Not with his finger, she realized with a jolt of alarm, but with the cold muzzle of a gun.

"It's a trick question, Miss Richland."

Hearing her name spoken by a complete stranger sent a chill snaking down her spine. She quickly scanned the area.

Her pulse accelerated when she realized no other people occupied the sidewalk save for old Manney Black tending his fruit stand on the next block, and she knew he was practically deaf.

Riley, obviously sensing her fear, began growling softly, deep in this throat.

"There is no forgiveness...only vindication. Sinners must atone for their sins. And when they're not man enough to do it themselves, someone else must pay for them, just like Jesus died on the cross for the salvation of mankind."

"Who are you?" She ventured a look over her shoulder, but only managed to glimpse the sleeve of the man's grey, pinstriped suit before he pressed the gun more firmly against her back. "What do you want?"

"Justice, Miss Richland, but I'll settle for revenge."

Riley's growl deepened, and he bared his teeth.

"I'd keep that mutt in line if I were you," the man advised. "I'm not opposed to shooting an animal."

"Riley, hush," she commanded. Thankfully, the dog obeyed.

"Or a person, for that matter," the man added as an apparent afterthought, but his voice told her he meant it.

"He'll behave. I promise." At least, she hoped so, for Riley's sake. "Please, don't hurt him."

"It's very admirable, Miss Richland, fretting over your guide."

He pushed her forward. Holly splashed through the puddle, dragging Riley with her, as the man's words echoed in her brain. *Fretting over your guide.*

Your *guide.* The guy thought she was blind, and she was more than willing to perpetuate that belief. It might give her the upper hand later...If she lived until later. Why didn't she listen to Ash and stay put?

"But I should think you'd be more worried about yourself right now."

"Who are you?" she asked again, a quake in her voice.

"Why, Miss Richland, I'm hurt. I truly am. Did you forget my notes and gift so easily?"

She froze. He was the one who sent her the music box. Dear Lord, Ash was right. Why didn't she listen?

The man grabbed her arm and jerked her along. Her skin crawled at his touch, and her heart began pounding a frenetic tattoo in her ears as he led her toward a nondescript white van parked on the side of the road ahead. A rapist van, she thought. Rapists always drive white vans. Her heartbeat quickened to a violent pace.

He pulled her to a stop behind the van and opened the back doors. Holly was finally able to get a look at his face, for all the good it did her. She'd never seen him before in her life.

"Get in," he ordered.

Panic surged through her veins. If she stepped inside the van, she knew she had a very slim chance of stepping back out of it alive.

"What do you want?" she asked, stalling for time to think up a plan, a way out of this mess. "What did I do to you?"

"You?" The man shook his head. "Nothing. You did absolutely nothing." He yanked her forward and shoved her toward the open van.

Holly couldn't stop the small cry that escaped her lips when her knee collided with the rear bumper. Thrown off balance as she was, it was easy for him to push her inside. She toppled forward, hitting her head on the metal floor. Riley barked and advanced on the man.

"Riley, come!" she called frantically, terrified for the dog's safety. The shepherd stopped moving, but his hackles were up, and he continued to bark. "Riley!" she repeated desperately, pressing a hand to her throbbing temple. "Come!"

Finally, the dog obeyed and jumped into the van. The man smiled smugly, as if he never doubted he'd eventually have his way. He closed one door, then stopped to stare at her.

"Pity it has to end this way, Miss Richland. You're a very lovely woman." His gaze played down the length of her bare legs, and she shuddered. "But as I said before...someone has to pay." With that, he slammed the door shut and locked it.

Holly tried the door, but it wouldn't open and there weren't any windows in the back. Whirling around, she frantically searched for an escape route. Her heart sank when she spotted the wire mesh partition separating her from the front of the van...and freedom.

Ash scoured every inch of his neighborhood, but there was no sign of Holly. Reluctantly admitting to himself she'd probably gone to the school to work with that damn dog, he jogged back to his apartment to call Paige, since he'd forgotten his phone when he rushed out the door.

He was halfway up the stairs when he spotted the note taped to his door. Taking the remaining steps two at a time, he ripped it off and read the inscription.

I've got her.

Three simple words and his world came crashing down around him. Holly. The bastard had Holly.

The telephone ringing inside galvanized him into action. He yanked the door open, flew to the kitchen and snatched the phone from the table before the third ring.

"Where is she?" he demanded hotly.

"Hi, my name is Rich. Would you like to save money on your Internet bill?"

Ash let out a roar of frustration and hurled the phone against the wall. Only after it hit with a satisfying crash and broke apart did he realize what he'd done. Now there was no way for the kidnapper to contact him. Seething with rage, he spun and knocked the table over, then stormed out of the apartment.

Ash drove to the police station like a madman possessed, the wind whipping the hair around his unprotected head. Helmets took too long to put on, and Holly might not have the time to spare.

He parked his bike by the red curb in front of the building and charged up the stairs. This was the last place he wanted to be, and his former captain the last person he wanted to talk to, but he didn't have a choice. Holly was missing, and he was forced to admit he didn't have clue one as to who had taken her, except possibly Jetzel.

And even if Jetzel was behind it, he'd still need some backup. Stellar Incorporated was too powerful a force to take on alone.

Ignoring the secretary, who looked genuinely surprised to see him, he made his way through the maze of desks. The blinds covering the huge windows of the back office were open, and he spotted Captain Lethcowitz sitting at his desk, animatedly gesturing while he talked on the phone.

Ash opened the door and barged inside before the captain could even acknowledge him. He expected the look of incredulity when the older man looked up. After all, it was only a handful of days ago he'd sworn never to set foot inside this building again.

"Lucille? I'll have to call you back." The captain hung up

the phone and gave him a once over. "Still haven't cut your hair, I see."

Ash ignored the jibe. "Don, I need your help."

"I must not have heard you correctly. Sounded to me like you were about to ask me a favor, even after walking out of here last week without so much as a day's notice."

"Dammit, Don, don't be an ass."

"Now, hold it right there, Malone." The captain stood, placed his hands on his desk and leaned forward menacingly. Every inch of his two-hundred twenty pound frame boasted solid muscle, a fact he often used to intimidate people. "Just because your father and I were friends doesn't mean you can waltz in here and insult me. I don't take crap from my team, and I definitely won't take it from you."

Ash nodded silently. The captain was right. He owed him too much to be treating him disrespectfully. Whoever murdered his father had never been caught. His grandfather and Don provided the stabilizing forces he needed to cope. He wouldn't have made it through the ordeal without the two men, and there was no one he would rather have seen replace his father as captain than Don Lethcowitz.

"You're right. I'm sorry."

The captain smoothed his mustache with his thumb and forefinger as he studied Ash thoughtfully. "What's the matter? I'm guessing it's something pretty bad to bring you back here."

"A woman's been kidnapped." He took a deep breath, burying his emotions. "A friend of mine."

"A friend?"

"A close friend," he amended. "Holly Richland. I think she was taken because of me."

"Why?"

A simple enough question, but he didn't have the slightest notion where to begin his explanation.

"Captain Lethcowitz?" A young officer stuck his head inside the doorway. "I'm sorry to bother you, sir, but there's a call for Detective Malone." He glanced warily at Ash. "The caller says it's a matter of life and death."

Holly.

Lethcowitz studied Ash before telling the young officer to patch the call through to his office and run a trace on it. When the phone rang a moment later, Ash answered it by hitting the speaker button, so they could both listen.

"This is Malone."

The smug voice on the line boiled his blood. He'd recognize that leisurely, complacent tone anywhere.

"Well, well, Detective Malone. I must say I am a little surprised to find you at the police station. I was under the impression you quit the force after that young girl died."

Ash narrowed his eyes. "You know how rumors spread. What do you want, Frankie?"

"Very impressive. I'm flattered you remember me, but I believe the correct question would be, what do *you* want, Detective?"

"You know damn well what I want."

Frank Desmond laughed. The sound was pure evil. "You're right. I do. She's very lovely, your friend. Very fragile, though, I'm afraid. She bruises quite easily."

Ash clenched his teeth so tightly his jaw hurt. He knew Desmond was baiting him, and he wasn't going to give the bastard the satisfaction of showing his anger, no matter how badly he wanted to rip the phone out of the wall, find him and wrap the cord around his neck.

"Where is she?" He ground the words out.

"With me, of course. I find I'm enjoying her company

immensely, and I believe she's starting to appreciate me as well."

Biting the inside of his cheek until he tasted blood, Ash tried to stay calm. He had to remain in control of his emotions for Holly's sake. "Aren't you going to tell me where you've taken her, Frankie? Isn't that why you called?"

"I called to make you suffer like I did after I lost my mother," Desmond said in a placid, devil-may-care tone, as if his emotions had been severed. Psychopath through and through. "But since you're so insistent, I'll give you a little hint, just to be sporting. You took a walk by this place—you, your lady friend, and that mutt of hers—right before she saved your worthless hide."

Instantly, Ash began replaying the day of the accident in his mind. "That's all I get? Frankie, cut me some slack."

Desmond laughed. "Detective, if I gave you any more slack you'd hang yourself with it."

"Frankie?"

No answer.

"Desmond?" The dial tone clicked through the line and he immediately looked to Lethcowitz. "Did we get it?"

The captain shook his head.

Ash slammed his fist onto the desk. "Dammit!"

"Fill me in, Malone. We're not talking about the same Frank Desmond who owns Stellar Incorporated, are we?"

He nodded absently, absorbed in his thoughts. *You took a walk by this place...right before she saved your worthless hide.* It couldn't be that easy, could it?

"He's what, in his early forties?"

Ash nodded again, not really paying the captain much attention until Lethcowitz swore out loud.

"What?"

"He's Mack Desmond's son."

"Who?"

"Mack Desmond. He was a small time embezzler. Your father put him away about ten years ago. He was killed in prison and his wife went off the deep end and OD'd on sleeping pills. His son must blame you for her death."

"That's ridiculous. Why would he blame me and not–" Ash stopped abruptly. His heart slammed against his chest so forcefully, he was certain it must have left an impression. "My God."

"What?"

"He killed Dad."

Lethcowitz shook his head. "Harry was shot in a robbery."

"That's what Desmond wanted us to think." His hands balled into fists. "He killed Dad and now he's got Holly."

"I think you're off base about Harry, but the guy does seem to have your girlfriend." Lethcowitz fingered his mustache. "The only question is where?"

"In an abandoned building in Pete's neighborhood."

"What?"

"That's what the clue meant." He started pacing back and forth in front of the desk. "But it's too damn easy."

"Maybe it was supposed to be. You know as well as I do these wackos thrive on attention. They get off on making the police jump through hoops. This is probably just the first trick he's got set up, but obvious or not, we still can't ignore it." Lethcowitz retrieved his blazer from the back of his chair and put it on. "I'll take a team out there myself and send one to the Stellar offices as well."

"Good idea. Let's get moving."

The captain placed a restraining hand on Ash's arm. "Hold on, hotshot. You're not going anywhere."

"Try to stop me."

"This is police business," Lethcowitz said pointedly. "The police will handle it. You're a civilian now, remember? You can't go with us."

"The hell I can't." Ash moved to go around him, but the captain sidestepped into his path.

"I'll throw you in jail if I have to, Malone."

"I'd like to see you try."

The captain stuck his head outside his office door and shouted, "Tanner! Whalen! Get in here! Now!"

Within five seconds, two of the biggest hulks Ash had ever seen—and also the toughest cops he'd ever worked with —were flanking Lethcowitz. Still, he might have rushed them, if they weren't holding guns. Especially Whalen. He was the deadliest shot in the precinct.

"In case I didn't make myself clear," the captain began, "civilians do not tag along on police business."

Ash eyed the three men blocking his path and snarled, "Then give me back my damn badge."

"Only if you give me your word you'll keep it," Lethcowitz countered. He walked to his desk, opened the bottom left drawer, reached inside and pulled out a leather billfold. When he tossed it onto the top of the desk, the flap opened up to reveal a badge situated above Ash's ID card. "Your choice, Malone. Take it or leave it."

Ash stared at the shiny metal shield. Under the fluorescent lights of the office, it seemed to wink in challenge. Picking up the badge would mean facing his nightmares head on. Letting it lie would mean abandoning Holly.

No contest. Devil be dammed. Ash snatched the billfold from the desk. Without a word, he turned, elbowed his way through the human wall blocking the doorway and stalked out.

Dressed in full body armor, sitting in the back of the SWAT van with his team members, Ash oddly felt as if he'd come home. Of his fourteen years on the force, he'd spent the last eight working with Jack and the four men seated next to him. He trusted them with his life, and now he was entrusting Holly's to them as well.

The van stopped a block away from the abandoned building. Ash got out and put in his ear piece. After briefly conferring with Lethcowitz, whose men were blocking off the street, he ordered his team into place. They automatically dispersed, the years of working together making it unnecessary for him to assign positions.

Whalen, the sharpshooter, went high. Tanner headed left, Garcia right, and Fuzzy moved around back. Jack would've stayed close to Ash so the two of them could cover each other as they assessed the situation and attempted to move in. Only this time, Ash would be going it alone, since Jack still hadn't responded to his text. Deep down, he couldn't blame him. After all, how many men would want to trade their son's sixth birthday party for the possibility of getting killed?

Flanked by two other police cars, Lethcowitz drove toward the building and parked across the street from its front door. The boards had been yanked away to litter the sidewalk, confirming Ash's suspicion that Desmond, or someone, was inside.

He watched from a distance as the captain pulled out his bull horn in preparation for attempting contact. Lethcowitz and his men were the decoys. Hopefully they'd create the diversion he needed to slip inside unnoticed.

Lethcowitz was lifting the bull horn to his mouth when a

car broke through the road block and skidded to a stop next to the SWAT van.

"Who is that?" Lethcowitz's voice crackled in his ear.

"I don't know." Ash didn't recognize the black Toyota Camry. "But I'll find out."

He moved in on the stranger who emerged from the Toyota. The man was bending over, so he couldn't see his face. When he racked the slide back on his gun and let it snap forward into place, the man froze at the sound.

"That's a hell of a welcome," the man said, slowly straightening to a standing position.

Ash took in his rangy build and military style haircut, then lowered his gun and removed his finger from the trigger.

"Jack, you almost got yourself killed. Whose car is that?"

"I was blocked in," he explained as he turned around. "This is Kenny Dietrich's mother's car, so don't go shooting any holes in it."

"She let you drive her car?"

Jack's mischievous grin answered the question for him.

Ash raised an eyebrow before turning his head toward the mic attached to his vest. "It's Fallon."

"Took his sweet time getting here. Let me know when you're ready."

Jack fastened the last Velcro strap on his bulletproof vest. "Ready."

"Thanks for coming," Ash said in a low voice.

Jack gave a short nod.

"Ready when you are, Captain."

Lethcowitz didn't acknowledge.

"Captain?"

Glancing toward the building, Ash saw everyone gathered around Lethcowitz's car with the captain seated inside.

"What's going on over there?" Jack asked.

Ash shook his head, an uneasy feeling creeping down his spine. "Captain, what's up?"

There was another long pause before Lethcowitz finally answered. "Better get over here. He's on the line, and he wants to talk to you."

Ash sprinted the distance with Jack following closely behind. When he reached the car, Lethcowitz handed him the cell phone.

"It's Malone. What do you want, Frankie?"

His answer was simple and to the point. "You."

"I'm here."

"Good. Now I want you unarmed and inside the building...just you."

Ash hesitated. The kidnapping procedure he'd followed religiously for the last eight years forbade trading other people for hostages, because no one usually ended up alive.

"What's the matter, Detective?" Desmond sneered. "Don't you care enough to trade your life for hers?"

He did, and he'd do it in a heartbeat. "Why are you doing this, Frankie? Your mother's dead, but so is my father. Doesn't that make us even?"

Desmond sighed heavily. "One minute your powers of perception amaze me and then the next you say something completely asinine like that. This has nothing to do with my mother. True, your father paid for her death, as he should have, but this..." He drew an audible, measured breath. "This is between you and me, and it's strictly business."

"What business?"

"I'm through chatting, Detective. Am I going to have to kill Miss Richland or not?"

Ash gritted his teeth together. He felt a trickle of sweat slide down his temple as a chill raked over him. He had to ask, but even forming the words made his gut twist. "How do I know you haven't killed her already?"

Desmond laughed, the sound like fingernails on a chalkboard to his frayed nerves.

"You don't."

CHAPTER FOURTEEN

Sitting on the filthy, decaying carpet, her hands tied behind her back, Holly watched her kidnapper hang up the phone. He wanted to kill Ash, and given the opportunity, she had no doubt he would.

That's why she was still alive. She was the chunk of cheese in his game of cat and mouse. If Ash tried to save her, the kidnapper would kill him. If he ignored the demands and stayed outside like she prayed he would, the man would kill her. She knew it. She could see it in his eyes, in the cruel curve of his lips.

Don't you care enough to trade your life...?

She did. She would. She'd die a thousand times over if that's what it took for Ash to live.

The realization made her breath catch. She knew she was in love with him. She just never understood how much until now.

The man turned to face her. Holly averted her eyes before he saw her studying him. He still thought she was blind, and she intended to keep it that way. If she ever managed to work her hands free, that belief might give her the edge she desperately needed to escape.

He strolled toward her, stopping a few feet in front of her, and she stared at his black shoes. A thin layer of dust coated them, dulling their shine. They appeared almost fuzzy in the dim surroundings. Since the electricity had been shut off ages ago, the only light in the building was the sunlight sifting through the boarded up windows, diffused by the dust and cobwebs.

"Don't worry, Miss Richland. Your prince charming will come to your rescue soon."

"You sound pretty sure of yourself," she said. "Especially since he's not my prince charming. He's not even my boyfriend. In fact, I've only known him a few days."

The man laughed. Full out, no holds barred laugh-til-you-cry laughter. The sound echoed throughout the empty hotel room. It made her shiver and caused Riley to start growling.

"You're a pitiful liar, Miss Richland, but quite amusing nonetheless."

He walked past her, just out of Riley's reach. The dog strained as far forward as his anchored leash would allow and began barking furiously. The man chuckled, lifted a foot and shook it. Riley went nuts.

"Riley, stop it," she ordered. True, the man was deliberately teasing the German shepherd, but she wouldn't put it past him to pull out a gun and shoot the dog for barking either, whether or not he instigated it. "Riley!"

When the barking subsided to a low growl, the man apparently grew tired of the game. He walked back to Holly, knelt down beside her, and without warning, fisted her hair and yanked her head back. She gasped, then bit her lip to keep from crying out further as tears trickled from the corners of her eyes.

"Are you praying now, Miss Richland? Praying for your lover to save you from your fate?" The man framed her face with both of his impossibly soft hands and wiped the tears away with his thumbs. "It won't help, you know," he stated calmly, his breath fanning her face. "Nothing will."

He ran a finger lightly across her lips. Holly tried to jerk away, but he held her fast.

"Such a pretty mouth." He moved closer, until his own mouth was a breath above hers.

"I do hope you scream," he whispered. "It'll be so much more dramatic when I make him watch you die."

"Hell no! You are not stepping foot inside that building. We don't do trades."

Ash glared at the captain before removing his gun from its holster and placing it on the hood of the squad car. "It's not your decision to make."

"The hell it's not. I'm your commanding officer."

His tactical duty belt and second firearm hit the roof of the car with a heavy thud. "I don't care."

"That's it. Cuff him, Fallon."

Without warning, Ash snatched up his gun and whirled around. Jack froze when the sights lined up with his nose.

"Ash, be reasonable," he stuttered. "You won't do Holly any good if you're dead."

"I won't do her any good sitting on my ass, either." He gripped the gun tighter. "Back off, Jack."

"Malone, you could be brought up on charges for this," the captain warned. "You'll lose your badge."

"Now there's a threat."

Ash eased away from the car and started backing up

toward the building. He kept his sights on his best friend until he stepped onto the sidewalk in front of the door.

"Sorry, Jack. I have to do this." With that, he slipped inside the building.

Standing next to the doorframe with his back against the wall, he heard Lethcowitz swearing up a blue streak outside. He couldn't blame the captain. Ash knew as well as he did this was a stupid move. Maybe he would get himself killed, but what did it matter? He wouldn't be able to live with himself if he let Desmond hurt Holly.

Ash scanned the interior of what used to be, if his grand-father was correct, one of Denver's nicer hotels. Now it was one of the nicer rattraps, he surmised, wrinkling his nose in disgust. The place reeked of stale air, rodents, filth and mildew.

To the left, the check-in counter stood before a wall of spider-infested cubby holes, judging from the tangle of webs covering them. He took in the shredded, moth-eaten velvet curtains, crumbling stone fireplace and scattered pieces of dilapidated furniture before focusing on the scuffed footprints leading to a curved stairway on the far left.

They were upstairs. And judging from the patterns in the dust-covered floor, Holly had walked there herself. That meant she was still alive. Or at least she was when they got here. Thank God.

Ash bent over and stashed his gun inside his right boot. Luckily, he'd grabbed his .22 and not the .9mm, so it was small enough to fit. He pulled his pant leg down to conceal the weapon and stood. He knew he was taking a chance in bringing a gun—especially if Desmond found it before he had the opportunity to use it—but his gut told him he'd be taking more of a chance if he left it behind.

Straightening, he steeled his resolve and called out, "Desmond?"

"How nice of you to join us. Did you leave your guns and friends outside?"

The voice sounded distant, but not far enough to be two flights up. Second floor, he concluded. They're on the second floor. He stuck his head outside the door and waved two fingers in the air until he saw Jack nod.

"I'm alone," Ash confirmed before lying through his teeth, "and unarmed."

"Then by all means, Detective, come up and join the party."

"Ash, don't!" Holly yelled, then stopped abruptly.

He heard the slap, and his blood began to boil. Riley started barking. He clenched his hands into fists, wishing with everything in him that Desmond's neck was in his grasp. The bastard. If there was one mark on Holly...

"Are you coming, Detective? Your girlfriend's getting impatient."

"Let her go, and I'll come up."

Desmond laughed. "Do you really think I'm that stupid? I'll let her go when you're standing in front of me and not a moment before."

Ash cursed under his breath and cautiously mounted the stairs. He'd dealt with too many lunatics over the years to believe Desmond would keep his word and release Holly. No, the only way either of them would be walking out of this situation alive was if Desmond didn't.

The stairway curved by a long hallway that branched into two others. At least twenty doors flanked the first hall, nearly every one of them open. It was hard to see clearly with the only light coming from a broken, partially boarded window at the end of the hall and muted glimmers of light from a couple of rooms.

"Like shooting fish in a barrel," he muttered. "Desmond?"

"Last door on the right, Detective."

Or seventh door on the left, for all he knew. The voice wasn't close enough to be in the first few rooms, but other than that, he couldn't tell for sure where it was coming from. The damn place echoed like a cavern, despite all the walls.

Left with no alternative, Ash began moving down the hallway. He was careful to stay close to the wall, only pausing when between doorways.

Reaching the last door before the hallway intersection, he took a deep breath and slowly stepped inside. Instantly, Desmond's gun locked on him.

"Detective Malone, so glad you could join us. But I'm afraid you're going to have to lose the vest...unfair advantage."

Ash reluctantly took off his bulletproof vest and let it drop to the floor with a *thud*. Slowly turning toward Desmond's voice, he spotted Holly.

Anger sparked through him as he took in her appearance. She looked like hell. Her right knee was cut and bleeding, and her arms had bruises from where Desmond had grabbed her. The previously healed wound on her forehead was torn open, dried tears streaked her face, and the corner of her mouth boasted fresh blood.

"Are you okay?" He mouthed the words more than spoke them.

She looked up at him from her position on the floor and gave a reassuring nod. She also pulled her hands from behind her back for a split second, then quickly replaced them before Desmond saw.

God, he loved that woman. The intensity of his feelings nearly knocked him on his ass. Anyone else would've been too scared to think straight, yet Holly had kept her wits about her and managed to get her hands free without Desmond realizing it.

"I'll kill you for this, Desmond." His words weren't so much a statement as a promise.

Desmond pursed his lips into a frown. "Temper, temper. You don't want to ruin Miss Richland's chance of staying alive, do you?"

"I'm here like you wanted. Let her go."

"What's the magic word?"

Ash narrowed his eyes. "Please," he ground out through clenched teeth.

"You know, that didn't sound quite sincere to me."

Desmond stepped closer to Holly. Doing so provided Ash with an unobstructed view of the German shepherd tied to a radiator on her right. Riley was systematically gnawing on his leash. He quickly looked away so as not to draw Desmond's attention.

'Atta boy, he praised silently. With Riley free, it would be three against one. Well, three against two if he counted Desmond's automatic, but all he needed was a few seconds to retrieve his own gun and the odds would get better.

"In fact," Desmond continued, oblivious to the dog's actions, "that was so unconvincing; I believe I'll have to kill you both."

That did it. Gun or no gun, the guy was going down. Ash tensed, preparing to attack. He exchanged a quick glance with Holly, and she slowly started getting to her feet. They could hit him at the same time. And even if the gun did go off, he rationalized, Desmond was aiming at him, so Holly wouldn't be hit.

"Get up very slowly, Miss Richland or Detective Malone dies."

She froze, her panicked gaze darting to Ash. "What?"

"You heard me. Get up and move over here slowly or I'll kill your boyfriend."

"But I can't—"

Desmond jerked her to her feet and waved his gun in her face. "Did you really think I was stupid enough to fall for your blind act? I know you can see, Miss Richland. I know everything about you, but it was incredibly thoughtful of you to occupy yourself by pretending to be blind. You have no idea how much easier it is to control someone when she's already walking on egg shells."

Holly's jaw dropped. Ash saw his chance and reached for his gun. He stopped in mid-crouch, however, when Desmond wrapped his arm around her neck and pulled her in front of him.

"Look familiar, Detective?" Desmond pressed the muzzle of his gun against Holly's temple. "Or is this better?"

The floor dropped out from under him. Ash suddenly felt as if he was free-falling. The room spun from his control, and a wave of nausea overcame him as memories attacked from every direction.

Gina Lyons. Desmond had Gina Lyons.

He shook his head in disbelief and squeezed his eyes shut. A dog was barking somewhere in the distance, barely audible over the pounding of the blood in his ears. When he reopened his eyes, the background seemed to race away as the two figures glided forward into sharp focus. Desmond was still there, but Ash's heart skipped a beat when Gina Lyons melded into Holly.

"What's the matter, Detective? Never experienced déjà vu?"

"Why? Why did he kill her?"

"He didn't. The only one that caused her death," Desmond corrected, "was you. She would have lived to see her grandchildren if you hadn't interfered."

"Donald Craig was working for you."

Ash wasn't aware he'd spoken the thought aloud until Desmond responded, "Very good. That wasn't so hard, now was it? Losing the money Craig was bringing in, however..." Desmond shook his head. "That was difficult. It took six years to get him into a position to do me some good, and you ruined it. So you see, Detective Malone, you alone were responsible for that girl's death. Today, however, I'll be more than happy to perform the honors."

Desmond cocked his gun, and Holly screamed. The sound ricocheted around the room, setting a chain of events into motion. Almost simultaneously, Holly elbowed Desmond in the stomach, Riley lunged, snapping his leash in the process, and Ash pulled the .22 from his boot.

A shot rang out. Holly screamed again, and Ash tasted bile in the split second before he whirled on Desmond and fired. At literally the same moment, Desmond's second shot knocked him off balance. White hot pain shredded his shoulder. He stumbled backward and fell against the wall, the impact forcing the air from his lungs and the gun from his hand.

"Ash!"

Holly practically threw herself on him, which didn't make breathing any easier. He didn't know if he'd hit Desmond or not.

"That fumble cost you a point, Detective."

Holly shifted around too look behind her, affording Ash a clear view. Desmond appeared unscathed. He picked up the discarded .22 and shook his head disapprovingly.

"Perhaps you'll do better in the second half." With Ash's gun in tow, Desmond smiled, turned and walked leisurely from the room.

"Oh my God, Ash, are you okay?"

He coughed and pushed himself away from the wall with his good arm. The movement ignited a fire in his left; pain shot down it and along his collarbone. He clenched his right hand over the wound and tried to ignore the burning as he faced Holly.

"I'm fine. Are you—?"

"Yes, but Riley's been shot."

He turned to see the German shepherd lying prone on the ground, whimpering softly.

"What're you doing?"

He struggled to his feet despite Holly's grip on his shirt. "I'm going after him."

"What? Are you crazy? You can't! He's probably still out there."

"I'm sure he is. No way he'd leave without finishing us off. This was just act one. He obviously wants me to follow him for act two."

"Which is why you can't. We'll find another way out."

"There isn't one. Besides, didn't you hear what he said? If I don't stop him now, he'll be back. Do you want to go through this all over again?"

"I won't let you go," she cried frantically, wrapping her arms around his neck.

Ash winced at the pain when she bumped his shoulder, then kissed her fiercely. "I've got to. Take care of Riley." Pushing her back, he ducked into the hallway.

"Ash!"

Holly's desperate cry tore through his soul, but he couldn't allow himself to go back to her. He'd meant what he said about Desmond not giving up. If he didn't stop him now, Holly would never be safe.

He studied the chaotic footprints on the floor, trying to decipher which direction Desmond had gone. It wasn't hard to figure out—an arrow was drawn in the dust.

Before heading in the direction it pointed, he bent and picked up a broken board from the floor to use as a weapon. His shoulder felt as if it was being eaten away by fire ants, but he couldn't let the pain stop him. Clenching his teeth, he pressed forward cautiously. He knew he was walking into a trap, but there wasn't any other way. He'd just have to remain alert and try to avoid it.

Ash wasn't even surprised when he smelled smoke. He knew Desmond wasn't above torching the place.

"Are you running away, Desmond?" He quickly scanned the room to his left before continuing past the open doorway. "I thought you wanted to finish this."

He was halfway down the hall now. Smoke hung in the air. A crash behind made him whirl around.

Nothing.

Damn, he'd give anything to have his gun right now.

Ash coughed as he moved into the thickening smoke. After a few more measured steps, he heard the dull roar of fire.

"Desmond?" He began descending the flight of stairs at the end of the hall. "If you intended to burn us alive, you should have started a fire in the room. I have plenty of time to get Holly out."

"Maybe." Desmond appeared at the bottom of the stairway holding some sort of detonator. "But who said I'm going to kill her with fire?" He flipped a switch and an explosion behind Ash rocked the building.

"Holly!"

Panic fired his reflexes as he sprinted back the way he'd come. Before he reached the top of the stairs, however, they blew into a million pieces.

Holly had just taken off her T-shirt and pressed it against Riley's side to try to slow the bleeding when the explosion hit. She automatically threw herself over the dog, but the ceiling didn't cave in like she expected. Luckily the blast wasn't close enough to have hit them directly...but what about Ash?

A second explosion drew a scream from her that resembled Ash's name. She had to find him. They had to get out of here before the entire building came down on top of them.

"Riley, get up!" she shouted frantically, tugging at the dog's collar.

The dog flailed around, whimpering and crying, but couldn't get to his feet.

"Ash!" she shouted toward the doorway, then turned back to the dog. "Riley, please! Get up! We've got to get out of here."

This time, the shepherd merely lifted his head off the floor.

"Ash!" she called again, but no answer. "Don't give up," Holly ordered the dog. "Riley, don't you dare give up!"

He looked at her with his big brown eyes, panting short, quick breaths, but didn't attempt to move.

"Riley, damn you! I won't leave you! *Get up!*"

Holly grasped the dog's harness and pulled with all her might. When he finally struggled to his feet with her help, she wrapped her arms under him and lifted. Her arms and back straining, she somehow managed to heft him part-way off the ground. Maybe it was desperation that gave her the strength to pick him up, or maybe it was love. She was closer to this dog than she was to her own parents.

Don't stop, her mind warned her. Whatever you do, don't stop to rest.

Holly carried Riley out of the room like a drunk stumbling in the dark.

"Ash!" she called again. Still no response and she couldn't see him anywhere. She didn't know where he was; didn't know if he was alive or dead. The stairwell to the left was a column of flames, so she went right, praying Ash was that direction too. She turned right again when the hallway split, because it appeared to have the least amount of smoke.

Riley started slipping from her grasp, but she refused to stop. If she put him down now, she knew she'd never be able to lift him again. So she continued to walk, the German shepherd's back legs dangling between her own as she waddled her way further down the hallway.

"We'll make it, Riley. We'll make it." She chanted the words like a mantra, drawing strength from them even though her muscles were throbbing and her lungs were burning as if she'd run a marathon.

It was stifling hot and smoke was billowing into the narrow space. Holly squinted and pressed on. She tried not to think of Ash, but the image of him lying dead somewhere kept taunting her.

"It's not true," she said, starting a new chant. "It can't be true."

Something crashed behind her. She panicked and moved faster. She could see the stairs now, could hear the sirens outside. Thank God. If she ever needed help, now was the time.

Holly was almost giddy when she reached the stairs,

despite the fact the smoke was so thick it stung her eyes and made it virtually impossible to see or breathe.

They were going to make it.

That was the last thought to enter her head before the third explosion struck.

Ash awoke with a coughing spasm that threatened to shake his body apart, or maybe it already had. He felt like he'd been drawn and quartered. Everything hurt. Even his hair.

"Malone? Hey, buddy, you're okay. You're going to be fine."

Ash knew that voice. It belonged to…"Jack?"

"Yeah, partner, it's me. You're fine."

He pushed away the oxygen mask even though his lungs were burning. "Holly?" he croaked out. The word was like sandpaper against his throat.

Jack didn't answer, and someone had put that damn mask on his face again. Ash knocked it off and struggled to a sitting position.

"Sir, you really should lie—"

"Where's Holly?" he demanded, frantically looking around. The air burned his eyes so much, tears spilled down his cheeks. "Jack, where is she?"

He tried to grab Jack and shake the answer out of him, but his left arm wouldn't budge. He made do with latching onto Jack's vest with his right.

"Dammit, tell me!"

Jack avoided his eyes. "She's still inside."

"What?"

"There was another explosion."

"Are they looking for her? Jack?"

He slowly shook his head. "The Fire Chief ordered everyone out of the building right after they found you...too much structural damage to be safe."

"Holly's still in there," Ash countered, attempting to stand.

"What do you think you're doing, Malone?"

"If no one else is going to find her, I am."

"Like hell."

Jack pushed Ash back against the car behind him. The sudden movement made his head spin.

"You're not going anywhere but the hospital."

"Not without Holly."

"We'll find Holly as soon as the chief gives the okay."

"That's not good enough!" He tried to stand again, but his injuries made it easy for Jack to overpower him.

"I'm sorry, man," he said, cuffing Ash's uninjured arm to the car door. "This is the way it has to be."

Ash tried to yank the door handle off the car, but couldn't. Trapped, he'd never felt more powerless in his entire life. Holly needed him, and he couldn't help her. Of all the horrible things that could happen, letting Holly down now was the second worst he could possibly imagine.

He didn't even want to think about the first.

CHAPTER FIFTEEN

Holly's eyes burned. She forced them open anyway and stared into darkness. Coughing, she swiped away the tears rolling down her cheeks and tried to concentrate. How long had she been here? She didn't know. All she remembered was dragging Riley down the hallway before the world shattered.

Something was jabbing her in the back. She moved gingerly and slid down a jagged hill only to stop abruptly. Stairs. She was on the stairs. That meant she had to have been thrown a good ten-fifteen feet. Her pulse accelerated.

"Riley?" she called weakly, choking on the thick smoke. "Where are you, boy?" Why was it so dark in here? She was never going to find him. "Riley?"

A coughing fit seized her, the fierce convulsions wracking her aching body, threatening to shred her throat. After it subsided, Holly started feeling around the stairs with her hands, but didn't touch fur anywhere. She did, however, burn her hand on a piece of metal, and if metal was hot enough to burn her, that meant the fire must be close.

She held her breath and listened carefully. Sure enough,

she heard the crackle and occasional popping sounds of the fire as it devoured the old dry wood in the building. Even though she couldn't see the flames, she could tell they were definitely close.

"Oh, God." Holly covered her mouth with her hand as a horrifying revelation hit her like a sucker punch to the gut. "Oh, dear God, no."

Fresh tears sprang to her eyes as she frantically looked around. Nothing but blackness met her gaze, and that's when she knew...

She was blind.

Her stomach suddenly lurched violently and she threw up. Panic and complete vulnerability smothered her, but she tried to fight the feelings back. She knew the fire was getting closer; she could smell the sulfur and burning wood. The pungent odor ripped another coughing round from her raw throat. She felt the heat on her face as she crawled around on the floor searching for Riley. She didn't know if she was going in the right direction or not. She'd climbed back up the stairs, but Riley could have been thrown all the way to the bottom of them for all she knew.

"Riley? Riley, where are you?"

Holly ran smack into some sort of board with her face. She cried out sharply when its jagged edge sliced her cheek. Pressing a hand to the wound, she reflexively backed up, nearly toppling down the stairs in the process.

Hopeless. This was hopeless. She was never going to find Riley or her way out. She was going to die in this building without ever telling Ash how much she loved him.

Pain, grief, and a dwindling supply of oxygen all ganged up on her at once. It was a crippling combination. Holly found herself curled into the fetal position before she even realized. It would be so easy to give up. She couldn't see, she couldn't move without hurting, and she could barely breathe.

Unfortunately, no matter how much a part of her wanted to, she couldn't quit now. Not when her life, Riley's and Ash's, if he was still alive, depended on her.

Ignoring the stabbing pains moving caused, she pushed herself back up onto her hands and knees. Her head struck another object as she did, but this one was warm and furry and whimpering in her ear.

"Riley!" She threw her arms around the dog's neck. "Oh, Riley, you're alive!"

The shepherd licked her face. His tongue was hot and dry, and he was panting heavily, wheezing slightly.

"Riley, we've got to get you out of here." She tried to draw him closer, rationalizing that if she could pull him onto her lap, she might somehow be able to slide down the stairs with him...if the bottom of the stairs was still there, that is. She had no idea whether the explosion had destroyed them or not.

Riley limped away from her grasp, then gingerly closed his jaws around her wrist and tugged softly.

"What, boy?"

The dog released her hand and swung his body around until his rear end bumped her. He whimpered and nosed her arm.

It took her a minute to catch on, but when she grasped the handle of the harness Riley still wore, he pulled forward as if urging her to follow.

Using the dog for balance, Holly struggled to her feet. She tightened her grip on the handle and whispered a silent prayer before saying, "Forward."

Riley started moving, slowly, jerkily. She could tell he was limping badly by the way the harness dipped and swayed. A few more steps and he stopped abruptly. She cautiously inched a foot forward to confirm her suspicion. They had reached the stairs.

Bracing a hand on the wall and using Riley for more support than she should have considering his condition, Holly gave the command and followed him forward.

It seemed like an eternity before they reached the bottom of the stairs, and in fact, it probably was at least fifteen minutes, because they were moving so slowly. She leaned down to pet the dog, praising him for the accomplishment and was dismayed by how hot his fur felt beneath her fingers. He was burning up, the gunshot obviously taking more of a toll than he was letting on.

Riley led her through a maze of fallen rubble and fire. She cupped a hand over her nose and mouth, trying to sift out the smoke, crying in pain whenever a flying ember burned her bare skin, voicing encouragement to the dog that was moving slower by the minute.

An odd roaring sound, different from that of the fire, caught her attention. It almost sounded like sandblasting, or a hail storm, or...

A strong, narrow spray of water hit her diagonally across the chest. After the initial shock wore off, Holly laughed out loud before a coughing spell seized her. The firemen must be spraying the outside of the building. That had to mean they were close, didn't it?

Another couple steps and Riley stopped again. Holly couldn't feel anything in front of her with her foot, so she urged the dog on. He wouldn't budge.

She raised her right arm and groped the surrounding air. Nothing. She lifted it higher, about eye level, and the back of her hand struck wood. Something was hanging down in her path.

"Good boy, Riley."

Bending down, she was careful to keep her hand on the protruding object as she walked underneath it. She was praising the dog again when whatever had been hanging down suddenly fell to the floor behind them with a crash. She screamed and bent over the dog, hugging him tightly. He was shaking violently, but she knew it wasn't because of the collapsing building. Even though Riley was hurting, his big canine heart wouldn't let him succumb to the pain.

Weeping uncontrollably and touched beyond belief by the dog's actions, she placed a kiss on his head before she straightened to a standing position.

"Forward."

Riley didn't disappoint. He limped on, and Holly followed without hesitation.

Before long, the collage of sounds coming from outside the building started sifting into individual pieces...sirens, water pummeling the walls, shouting. They became more and more distinct from the constant roar of the flames.

When that first blast of fresh air struck her, she started sobbing in relief. Relief turned to panic, however, when she was pulled off balance by the abrupt dive of the harness.

"Riley!"

Suddenly, hands were everywhere, pulling her away from the dog, lifting her when she tried to resist. Holly struggled against the cold, rubbery body that held her captive.

"Riley!...Riley!"

Didn't they realize Riley needed her? Didn't they understand?

"Holly?"

She froze at the sound of his voice, while her pulse simultaneously hit light speed. "Ash?" She somehow managed to wriggle free of the hands holding her and stumbled forward.

Ash caught her and drew her close. He kissed the top of her soot-covered head, then pushed her back so he could study her face and convince himself she was all right. Jack had uncuffed him when they saw Holly exit the building, but the handcuffs still hung from his right wrist. "Thank God you're safe."

Tears streamed down her face along with blood from a fresh gash across her cheek. "I thought you were dead. I mean, I didn't know—" She started coughing and her words broke off abruptly.

Two paramedics appeared, and Ash reluctantly released her to their care. She fought them tooth and nail, screaming for him not to leave her.

"I'm here," he assured her. "I'm right here."

"Ash? Where are you? Ash!"

Her terrified cries cut through him like knives.

"Holly, I'm here."

She choked on her tears, coughing and sputtering. "Where are you?"

The paramedics were holding her down. It took everything in him to keep from knocking them out of his way and gathering her back into his arms.

"Holly, you're safe," he promised her. "I'm here."

"Ash! Oh God, Ash! I can't see you! *I can't see!*"

Her frantic words hit like a bucket of ice water. "What?"

"I can't see!" she repeated as the paramedic placed an oxygen mask over her nose and mouth, muffling her crying.

Dazed, he watched the paramedics work. They gave Holly an injection and she quieted down, but her words rang through his head loud and clear. *I can't see.*

He felt numb. His shoulder didn't even hurt anymore. He felt absolutely nothing except the panic systematically crowding out every other emotion.

"Check her eyes," he ordered.

Both paramedics glanced in the direction of the guide dog, then back at him.

"We thought she was hysterical," one of them said. "You mean, she really isn't blind?"

Ash swallowed the fear rising in his throat and whispered, "God, I hope not."

CHAPTER SIXTEEN

"How long before we know for sure?"

Holly was thankful Ash asked the question, because for the life of her, she couldn't muster the courage to ask it herself. It was hard enough lying in this hospital bed waiting for the answer. Would she regain her sight or not?

"It could be hours or it could be days," Dr. Garrett informed them. "It depends."

"On what?"

Thank you, Ash. He was asking all the right questions.

"On the individual, the extent of the injury to the optic nerve," the doctor rattled off, "lots of variables."

"So what? Until then I just sit here and wait?" How much waiting could one person take? She was already going nuts waiting to hear about Riley's condition from the vet.

"I'm afraid so, Miss Richland."

She heard Dr. Garrett leave the room a moment later. In the hours she'd spent in Rose Medical Center, she'd learned the sound of his shoes. The nurses all wore those rubber-soled numbers so they were able to sneak up on her, but Dr. Garrett apparently preferred dress shoes, the kind that made a definite clack on the floor when he walked.

"I don't think I can do this, Ash," she whispered. For once she was grateful for the bandages covering her eyes, because they prevented him from seeing her tears. "I'll go crazy not knowing."

"No, you won't. I'll stay here and distract you."

Holly reached her hand out, intending to find and hold his. She accidentally bumped his arm instead and heard his sharp intake of breath.

"I'm sorry. Did I hurt you?"

"No. The pain killers are starting to wear off, that's all."

"How is your shoulder? It looked pretty bad."

"It looked worse than it was," he insisted. "The bullet made a clean exit. I'll be good as new in no time."

"Thank God." She sighed. "At least one of us will be."

"You'll be fine, Holly. I know you will."

She pressed her lips together, fighting for control over her emotions. "What if you're wrong?"

"I'm not."

"But what if you are?"

He didn't answer immediately. Instead, he lifted her hand to his lips and pressed a kiss into her palm before he spoke. "Then on that very remote chance—and I'm stressing the remote part here—you'll have to make do with the best guide dog in the business."

Riley.

"How is he? Have you heard?"

"He was still in surgery last time I checked. I left them my number. We'll have to wait until they call."

She let out a short, humorless laugh. "I hate waiting."

Ash squeezed her hand. "I know."

"I owe him my life. He can't die."

"He won't. Think positively, sweetheart."

Holly sniffed, then sniffed again. Ash leaned across her, so close she could smell the smoke that still clung to his hair. She heard the raspy sound of a tissue being pulled out of the box right before he leaned back and placed it into her hand. The kindness of his gesture made her cry even harder.

"Holly..."

"I'm sorry." She blew her nose. "I'm being stupid, I know."

"You're not."

"God, I'm such a hypocrite. I can't tell you how many times I've assured students at the school they can lead perfectly normal lives despite their blindness, and yet here I am; scared to death I'll never be able to do anything again. I know that's wrong. I mean, consciously I know it, but I still can't make myself believe it."

"Don't go getting ahead of yourself. We don't know anything for sure yet. Don't waste time worrying about something that might not even happen."

"But we have to talk about it. It'd change my life. It'd change us." The words slipped out before she could stop them. Mortified, she covered her mouth with her hands.

"Is that what you're worried about? Holly..." Ash captured both her hands in his and held them tightly. "It wouldn't make any difference between us."

She shook her head. "It would. You don't know."

"I do know. I'd still love you whether you could see or not. Hell, you wouldn't even be able to get rid of me if you learned how to cook."

"What did you say?"

"You can take cooking classes?" he teased.

"Ash."

She was surprised when his lips brushed across hers.

"I love you. Is that what you mean?"

"Do *you* mean it?"

"I wouldn't say it if I didn't."

She inhaled a choppy breath. "You'd better not."

When his mouth covered hers, Holly wrapped her arms around his neck, not caring if she never let go. She let her response tell Ash how she felt...wild—for him, passion-ate—about him. She put every ounce of love she could muster into that kiss.

They were both breathing heavily when their lips parted. She snuggled into him; tucked under his right arm with her cheek and hand resting on his chest. His heart was pounding so strongly, she was certain her hand must be bouncing.

"I love you too."

"What the hell do you think you're doing?"

Holly cringed at Ash's heated words, her guilty fingers grasping the end of the bandage wrapped around her head. She caught her bottom lip between her teeth.

"Can't I leave you alone for five minutes while I get a cup of coffee?" He stomped across the room.

"You were supposed to get lunch," she pointed out. "And nothing in a vending machine qualifies."

The hospital bed mattress sank under Ash's weight. "I forgot my phone. Obviously, it's lucky I did."

"Ash—"

"Holly, you know the doctor said you're supposed to leave those bandages on for at least a week."

She rolled the gauzy strip between her fingers, refusing to put it down. "I can't wait a week."

"Sure you can."

"No," she snapped, "I can't!" She'd run out of patience during the last two days. Not knowing whether she'd ever be able to see again was tearing her apart slowly, and she couldn't—she wouldn't—take it any longer.

"Holly..."

His soothing, everything-will-be-all-right tone pushed her over the edge. If the doctors didn't know whether she'd regain her sight or not, he sure as hell didn't.

"Dammit, Ash, they're not your eyes!"

Her voice echoed in the small, sterile room, and she was appalled by its bitter edge. None of this was his fault, yet here she was taking out her frustration and fear on him when he'd been nothing but loving and supportive the entire time.

"I'm sorry," she said finally. "But can't you understand I need to know now?"

The mattress lifted. Seconds later, she heard Ash's footfalls heading toward the door.

"I said I was sorry. Please don't leave."

He stopped walking. "I'm not."

She heard the door shut, followed by a soft click.

"What are you doing?"

"Turning off the lights."

Holly held her breath, afraid to jump to the wrong conclusion.

He walked toward her slowly, stopping next to the bed. She waited, but he didn't say anything.

"Ash?"

A heavy sigh.

"Ash?"

"Let me do that." He moved her hands away from the bandage. "Keep your eyes shut until I tell you to open them."

Mutely, she nodded. She honestly couldn't believe he was

189

giving in. And, if she were to be entirely truthful with herself, she almost wished he hadn't. What if she still couldn't see?

Cautiously, he began unwrapping the bandage. She felt it circling around her head, lifting her hair, brushing her nose. She inhaled the stale smell of antiseptic, heard the shallow breaths Ash took.

When there was barely a wisp of gauze left covering her eyes, Holly reached up and stopped his hand with her own.

"I'm scared," she whispered.

"Me too," he whispered back before unwrapping the last of the bandage. "Now, remember...keep your eyes closed."

The soft patches were lifted from her eyelids one by one. Holly had never felt more vulnerable in her life.

"Okay." Ash captured her hand in his. "Open your eyes slowly." He emphasized the last word.

Trembling, she tightened her grip on his hand as if it was a lifeline. She blew out the breath she'd been holding, drew in another shaky one and chewed on her bottom lip.

Finally, carefully, she opened her eyes. At first, she saw only darkness. Her breath caught in her throat and tears pooled in her eyes, then slipped down her cheeks when she blinked.

Gradually, however, the darkness transformed. Weak flecks of light began snowing around the outer edge of her field of vision. The black fluctuated to gray and then back, as if someone was playing with the control knob of a mood light.

"Well?" Ash sounded impatient.

She shrugged. "I don't know. I..."

Wait. Something moved. A ghost of an image burned into the blackness. She closed her eyes and opened them again. The ghost materialized into a shadowy form.

"I think..." She squinted. "Lift your arm."

A shadow moved through the snow causing a bark of laughter to escape her lips.

"I saw it!"

"You did?"

"I mean...well, I...I saw something," she amended. "A shadow, I think." Was she only imagining it? Did she want to see something so badly that her subconscious had conjured it up?

"There!" she shouted, pointing an accusing finger. "I saw it again."

Ash's voice was this side of ecstatic when he confessed, "I lifted my arm again."

"Oh, Ash, do you think...?" Holly was afraid to finish her question in case she might somehow jinx what was happening.

"Stay put," he ordered. "I'm going to get the doctor."

She heard him sprint toward the door, then back again.

He kissed her on the cheek. "Keep your eyes closed. I'll be right back."

After reprimanding Holly for taking off her bandages without his permission, Dr. Garrett examined her eyes.

"What exactly do you see?"

"Not much," she confessed. "Shadows...white dots, like when you get a camera flashed in your face and you see stars for five minutes afterward."

"What do you think, Doc?"

"It's promising. A little too early to tell anything for sure, but very promising. If," the doctor cautioned, "you keep your eyes wrapped for another week."

She sighed in relief and allowed herself a little smile. Dr.

Garrett wasn't the type to call something "very promising" if he didn't truly believe it was.

"I promise."

"And I promise to make sure she keeps her promise."

The telephone on the bedside table rang. Ash had barely said hello before Holly asked, "Is it the vet?"

"No." He sounded apologetic. "It's Jack."

Her good spirits took a nose dive. The longer it took to hear from the vet about Riley's condition, the harder it was for her to remain positive. Even though he'd made it through the surgery without any added complications, the vet had warned her not to be too optimistic.

It wasn't fair. Riley didn't deserve to die. He deserved to be teamed with a blind partner. He deserved to receive the medal of valor the Denver police department had decided to award him. He deserved to live.

Ash was still on the phone by the time Dr. Garrett finished applying new bandages to her eyes and left the room.

"Okay, Jack. Thanks for calling." He let out a huff of a laugh. "Yeah, I'll tell her."

"Tell her what?"

"That he's happy your sight's returning, but sorry I was the first thing you had to see."

Holly smiled in spite of herself. That shadowy blob was Ash, wasn't it? "And you've never looked better."

"Thanks," he grunted. "He's also thrilled about having two eyewitnesses at the trial."

"Trial? What do you mean?"

"They caught Desmond."

"They did?"

"Yeah." The bed sank under his weight. "Apparently his little diversionary explosions didn't work quite as well as he'd hoped."

"Thank God." She fell against him like a rag doll. Suddenly, every ounce of energy left her as the fear for their safety drained away.

Ash wrapped his arms around her, and she snuggled closer to his warm, solid frame. He smelled like freshly laundered cotton and ivory soap.

"I know it won't be pleasant, but you will testify, won't you?"

She didn't hesitate before answering, "Try to stop me." After what that man did to her and Ash, and especially Riley, nothing on earth could keep her away from the witness stand.

They sat on the hospital bed for a long while, wrapped in silence and each other's arms. When the ring of the telephone ripped through the quiet, Holly's heart skipped a beat and she stiffened.

"It might not be the vet," Ash cautioned.

Maybe not, she acknowledged silently. But if it was the vet, she wasn't sure she wanted to hear what he had to say.

EPILOGUE

"**F**riends, relatives, invited guests. We've asked you here today..."

Holly listened to the rest of the outdoor ceremony while her stomach quietly tied itself into knots. Perspiration beaded her forehead. Apparently, the sleeveless chiffon dress she wore was no match for the hot August afternoon, because she could feel it sticking to her back. They should have done this inside where there was air-conditioning. It was simply too hot out here.

Or maybe it was just nerves.

Through the sunglasses she was still required to wear whenever she was outside, she stole a glance at Ash. He stood beside her, perfectly calm.

How did he do it? She was a nervous wreck, and he looked relaxed enough to fall asleep.

He must've read her mind, because he chose that moment to smile down at her and give her hand a reassuring squeeze. Unfortunately, that only made her heart beat faster.

"I can't believe how nervous I am," she whispered,

leaning in closer, trying to absorb some of his strength. "What if he messes up?"

Ash chuckled softly. "How could he possibly mess up? He was trained by the best." She must not have looked convinced, because he added, "Have faith. He's come too far not to go all the way now."

Holly turned her attention back to the line of five guide dogs sitting to the right of the podium with their puppy raisers, patiently waiting to be officially presented to their new blind partners.

Riley was the last dog in the line. He looked so beautiful and healthy that her eyes teared up. In fact, to observers who didn't know better, they would never be able to tell the German shepherd had almost died three months ago, except for the patch of fur on his side that was slightly shorter than the rest. She was still amazed at how much faster dogs recovered than humans, but she was eternally grateful.

One by one, the graduating blind students stood when Carmen called their names, and the 4-H children who'd raised the dogs for the first year of their lives walked them over to their new partners. Even though Jimmy Kessler had to return Riley after only five months because his father was transferred unexpectedly, Holly had still invited him to present Riley to the young blind woman he was partnered with. After raising Riley herself for the remaining seven months before he entered his official training, she didn't think she'd be able to hand him over without breaking into tears.

Good thing Jimmy was able to accept her offer, because the flood gates burst when Riley's new partner took control of the harness.

Before she could even ask, Ash handed her a Kleenex. He draped his arm around her shoulders, which were shaking from the effort it took for her not to cry out loud, and pressed a kiss into her hair.

"Our boy's all grown up," he said when the ceremony was over.

Holly sniffed, but didn't trust her voice enough to respond verbally, so she nodded instead.

"I know you'll miss him, but he's got a good home. Anna's a sweet kid."

"I know she is. They're perfect together. It's just..."

"You'll miss him."

She nodded mutely, her face dissolving into tears. Ash pulled her closer and held her while the sobs wracked her body.

"How's she holding up?"

Holly heard Paige's question. She was grateful her friend had addressed Ash instead of her, because she didn't feel like talking right now.

"Better than I expected."

"Yeah, right. How do you think I found you? I just listened for the loudest crying and followed it."

"Shut up, Paige," Holly ordered, her face still buried in Ash's chest.

"It was a beautiful ceremony."

Surprised to learn that Paige wasn't alone, Holly turned around.

"So I lied," Paige said with a grin. "Jack and Elaine led me to you."

Embarrassed, Holly took off her sunglasses and wiped the tears from her face with the tissue. "I'm sorry."

"Don't be silly," Elaine said. "It's perfectly under-standable."

Jack nodded in agreement. "If it'll make you feel any

better, you're welcome to come over and watch Elaine bawl when Dylan starts first grade in two weeks."

Elaine elbowed her husband in the ribs, winning a watery smile from Holly.

"It was nice of you to come today. I appreciate it."

"We both do," Ash corrected, relieved to see Holly was apparently over her crying jag. He felt so helpless when she cried. That's why he'd made it his personal goal to never leave her side, so he could ensure she remained happy. Of course, there was also the minor fact he'd be miserable without her.

"Why don't we head inside?" Paige suggested. "Whatever the caterers delivered earlier smelled heavenly." She smacked her lips together to emphasize her point.

"We'll meet you in there."

Ash was impressed when Paige took the hint and left with Jack and Elaine instead of asking Holly why she didn't want to go inside yet. Although, come to think of it, he was wondering that very thing. At least, until he followed her gaze to where Riley stood beside Anna and her boyfriend a few feet away.

"Do you want to do this yourself?" he asked.

"No."

She held out her hand to him, and he saw the way it trembled slightly before he took it in his own.

Together, they walked over to the threesome. Holly congratulated Anna and the two women hugged. Ash shook the boyfriend's hand, then watched as Holly knelt before Riley. To her credit, Anna moved over to stand with her boyfriend and Ash, affording Holly a private moment with the German shepherd.

She scratched him behind the ear, the whole while whispering words only the dog could hear. Riley put his paw on her arm, and she covered it with her hand as silent tears spilled down her cheeks. Then she kissed the dog on the nose and hugged him fiercely. That's when Ash realized for the first time he was going to miss that damn dog too. After all, if it weren't for Riley, he would've lost Holly. He owed that mutt everything.

"You take good care of him," he told Anna.

"I will. I promise."

"And send us a text every once in a while, would you? Let us know how you're doing."

Anna smiled. "Of course."

Ash turned back to Holly. She was still hugging the dog, but gradually her grip loosened, and she pulled back to look into his eyes. Riley licked her nose, and she laughed despite her tears. Ash clenched his teeth together and swallowed hard.

She kissed Riley on the nose one last time, gave him one last scratch behind his ear, and slowly stood. Anna and her boyfriend walked over to meet her. The two women hugged again, then Holly turned around and made a beeline for Ash.

He folded her into his arms. "You okay?"

She nodded, but not with very much conviction. "I will be." She sniffed and licked a tear from the corner of her mouth with her tongue. "You're right. Anna's great. She'll be really good to Riley, and they're perfect together. He's supposed to be with her."

"I love you, lady."

She furrowed her eyebrows. "What?"

"You heard me." He tilted her chin up with his forefinger and kissed her tenderly. "I love you."

"Even when I look like this?" she asked, wiping a tissue across her nose.

"Especially when you look like this."

She eyed him crookedly. "Sometimes I worry about you, Ash."

"Then I guess you'd better stick close and keep me out of trouble."

"Ha! Nothing like a tall order. You do realize that could take quite a while."

"I'm counting on it."

Holly laughed, twined her fingers through his and led him toward the reception being held in the school. "Okay, but if I have to work overtime, I intend to get paid overtime."

"Name your price."

"You."

"Me?" He raised an eyebrow. "Honey, you've already got me."

"I do?" she asked coyly. "I wasn't sure."

Ash stopped abruptly and tugged on her hand. The spontaneous action caused her to fall back into his arms where he held her tightly. Lowering his mouth to hers, he kissed her with such love and conviction that she was clinging to him when their lips parted. "Are you sure now?"

"I think so," she teased.

"You *think* so?" He kissed her again, long and deep.

Holly sighed against his lips. "Maybe 'think' was a bad word choice."

"No maybe about it."

Again, his mouth claimed hers for a devastating kiss.

"What were we talking about?" she asked breathlessly.

He wiggled his eyebrows. "Skipping the party and going home?"

"We can't skip the party," she admonished, but her words were laced with regret.

"Okay." He knew this was important to her. Still, he

couldn't resist suggesting, "But let's only stay fifteen minutes."

Holly laughed. "Ash, get real. We're not staying a minute over ten."

She turned to him and smiled. The look was so suggestive; Ash knew...these were going to be the longest ten minutes of his life.

TO MY READERS

I just wanted to say thank you! I know you have a lot of book choices out there, so I'm grateful you took the time to read mine.

If you liked BLINDSIDED, I'd really appreciate if you could leave a review on Amazon. Even a sentence or two makes a huge difference to a new author! Reviews—and telling your friends—help other readers discover the book.

Don't forget to follow me on Facebook @ *Angela Taylor – Author* for info on upcoming books, giveaways and more. And feel free to drop me a line at angelataylor.romanceauthor@gmail.com. I'd love to hear from you!

Be sure to watch for the release of my next book, CHECK-MATE, coming early 2021!

I've included an excerpt, so you can check it out for yourself.

Thanks so much, and enjoy!
Angela

ABOUT THE AUTHOR
ANGELA TAYLOR

Angela was born in Montana and moved to Idaho when she was in the eighth grade. A huge animal lover, she's actively involved in dog rescue and volunteers weekly at her local shelter.

Aside from writing romance, she's an avid movie-goer who isn't above seeing a questionably bad flick just to satisfy her movie popcorn fix. In the past, she owned an entertainment company: writing, directing and performing murder mysteries and Wild West shows on the local train line and at private events. She's also a fan of professional motocross and knows every Hallmark Christmas movie by heart. Currently, she's considering founding a DCAA (Diet Coke Addicts Anonymous) support group.

Angela shares her rural home with two short, furry children, Remi and Ruby, and her husband, Dean, who probably won't be surprised she mentioned the dogs first.

Follow her on Facebook @ *Angela Taylor – Author*

<u>Available Soon</u>
Checkmate

CHECKMATE

No wedding ring.

Standing at the front of the restaurant, Billie Shayne couldn't stop herself from staring at his unadorned left hand. The familiar feeling of disappointment tried to worm its way into her body, but she shook it off.

Innocent until proven guilty, she reminded herself. Besides, lots of married men don't wear wedding rings.

And lots of married men do, her conscience quickly pointed out.

Rats! This wasn't going to be easy. Why did he have to be so darn handsome? Amend that. Why did he have to be so darn handsome and married?

Occupational hazard, her conscience answered.

Billie couldn't argue that one. She was definitely in the wrong line of work for meeting nice, eligible, single men. Not that she was looking. In fact, if she was to be honest, finding a man came right after cleaning out her junk drawer on her list of things to do, and locating a pair of scissors or a rubber band was just not that important.

Sneaking another look at her new "boss" from behind the stack of menus she was sorting, she made a mental note to bawl out her real employer, Mark, one more time for good measure. He could've at least warned her their client's husband was gorgeous. He also could've had the decency to not use her real name for this case.

"Billie..."

The deep baritone voice startled her, as it did every time he spoke.

Rats. Even his voice was gorgeous.

She somehow managed to conjure a smile before looking up to meet those devastating eyes of his. A soft, pale green, they were the most unique color she'd ever seen, and the dark fringe of lashes framing them only intensified the translucent hue.

"Yes?" Her softly husky voice sounded impossibly light and feminine compared to his. Well, at least that's something positive. She'd always considered her voice too low to be appealing. Why couldn't she sound like Reese Witherspoon, or...

"Would you please show Mr. and Mrs. Norris to table twelve?"

Billie had spent the better part of the afternoon memorizing the table numbers and floor plan of Montgomery's, but she hesitated just long enough to check the laminated map strategically taped to the hostess tabler before answering, "Certainly. Right this way, please."

She picked up two menus and led the elegantly dressed couple to their appointed table. Thanks to the cheat sheet Pam provided before going on maternity leave, she now knew where table twelve was.

After making sure the couple was comfortably seated, she

left them to ponder their dinner choices and started back toward the hostess table. She took her time, however, because he was still there.

Standing in his usual position between the hostess table and the front door, Royce Montgomery, owner of the five-star restaurant bearing his name, greeted another group of patrons. She had to admit it was a nice touch. Personally welcoming every customer made them feel important, flattered and pampered enough to come back, which they did. Weekend reservations at Montgomery's booked out weeks, sometimes months in advance.

He was impeccably dressed, she noted, in a black Armani suit which complimented his smoky good looks. He was clean shaven, and his raven hair was neatly styled, the sideburns freshly trimmed. Even though she thought his hair would look better finger combed, preferably by her own fingers, she couldn't argue one indisputable fact: the man was perfection with a capital "*P*."

Except, of course, for the fact he was married.

And he didn't wear a wedding ring.

"Out. Out, Mark. I want out," Billie demanded, pacing around her boss' office. She knew she was being unreasonable. This was her job, after all. Her chosen career. Well, almost. More like a detour chosen career until she could save up enough money to go to law school, but that was beside the point. The truth was this particular job made her uncomfortable. He made her uncomfortable. The last thing she wanted was to play decoy opposite Royce Montgomery.

Mark Davis, head of the CheckMate Detective Agency,

which specialized in matrimonial investigations, grinned indulgently. He slouched down in his battered Naugahyde chair, placed his left foot on his desk and crossed the ankle with his right before answering. "You've only been there one night. Give it a chance. Besides," he added, pausing to light a cigarette which replaced the one he'd just put out not five minutes ago, "I don't think things could've gone any better."

Billie wrinkled her nose. "Oh pu-leese! Aren't you forgetting the little matter of my name?"

He groaned, blowing out smoke in the process. "Are you still on that? I told you, it was a mistake. I'm sorry, but what could I do?"

"You could've corrected the situation," she accused, pointing a finger at him. "You should've told her it would be unethical—" She jabbed him in the chest. "—for me to use my real name on a case. Not to mention unprofessional—" Another jab. "—uncomfortable—" Jab. "—unfair—" Jab. "—and completely and totally stupid."

She jabbed him one final time to punctuate her point, and Mark rolled his chair back away from her, rubbing his chest. "Okay, okay, I get it. Jeez! I should've said something, but I didn't. It's water under the bridge. I can't change it now."

She started to argue, but moved aside an ashtray to sit on top of his cluttered desk instead. He was right. Besides taking her off the case, there was nothing he could do. Which reminded her... "I want out."

"No." His tone quickly drew her gaze as he crushed out his cigarette. Mark wasn't usually so forceful with her. Most of the time she had him wrapped around her little finger, and after she watched him for a moment, his face did soften. "I can't take you off the case now. Stephanie Montgomery made a mistake and gave her husband your real name. I know it'll be a little awkward for you, but let's not forget why she hired us."

Billie closed her eyes as shame washed over her. How could she selfishly be thinking of herself, when that man's poor wife was counting on her?

So what if she had to use her real name? She could deal with that. Who cared if she felt a little uneasy because she found the man attractive? She could deal with that too. What she couldn't deal with was letting that woman down. Stephanie Montgomery deserved the truth as to whether or not her husband was cheating, and Billie was going to get it.

"You're right," she conceded, retrieving the field notes she'd tossed onto his desk earlier. "I'll stay on the case."

"That's my girl."

"I'm not your girl," she reminded him for the umpteenth time. Still, she couldn't stop the grin tugging at the corner of her lips.

"Sure you are. You're all my girls," he replied, slipping into their well-worn verbal routine.

"Mark, your name is not 'Charlie.'"

"I know I'm not Charlie," he insisted, sounding as if nothing was more obvious. "You've seen me." Billie rolled her eyes. "And you're definitely not an angel—"

"Hey!"

"—but you know, you're my favorite."

"Yeah, yeah, yeah." She waved him off with feigned indifference, feeling much more at ease. Mark always could make her feel better. His big brother act had annoyed her when she first started working at CheckMate, but now she loved it. Mostly because it wasn't an act any longer. Billie knew he truly cared for her, and she really did think of him as the big brother she never had. More importantly, she'd come to trust him. In fact, he was the only man she did. "Tell it to someone who'll buy it."

~

Mark watched Billie leave his office with the promise of returning to Montgomery's. Since he was now alone in the room, he lit another cigarette and patted himself on the back. So what if he wasn't Charlie? James Bond was always more his style anyway.

Feeling quite smug, he took a long drag off his cigarette and attempted to blow a smoke ring, failing miserably. He scrunched his nose and sneered at the pathetic puff of smoke dissipating into the air, then reached for his phone and dialed.

"Hello?"

"Steph, it's me. She just tried to back out, but I talked her into staying on the case."

"Really?" The woman on the other end squealed, sounding like a five-year-old who'd just been given a pony. "Mark, that's wonderful. Do you think it'll work?"

He flicked the ash off his cigarette before taking another puff. "I don't know," he admitted, exhaling smoke. "She's not stupid, so I don't know how long we'll have before she catches on. But, with any luck, it'll at least take a few weeks."

"Gee, that's not very long. Maybe I could hint around to—Are you smoking?"

Mark inhaled sharply, causing the smoke to go down the wrong way. He started coughing, but tried his best to cover the sound. "What?" he choked out, his eyes stinging with tears. He crushed the cigarette into the ashtray on his desk and shoved it aside. "No."

"Mark Jacob Davis, you promised me you were going to quit."

Uh-oh, the middle name. That's never good. "I did," he stammered. "I will...I mean, I am. This is my first one today."

Be sure to pick up CHECKMATE
to find out what happens between Billie and Royce.

You won't want to miss it!

Made in the USA
Middletown, DE
31 December 2020

28180107R00119